# ROYALTY'S SAVAGE

### A NOVEL BY MARINA J

# ACKNOWLEDGEMENTS

MCP is the dopest publishing home I've ever been at. It feels like home and I feel like I have more family. Candice, thanks for being you and the type of publisher that you are. I truly appreciate you and all your guidance. Thank you so much. We LIT!!!

# DEDICATION

My books are always dedicated to my Super Six and my husband. I love you guys for always supporting me.

# CHAPTER ONE

## SAVAGE

Let me politic with ya right quick, ya' dig? Y'all met me as a young kid and watched me grow up a lil' bit. I was seventeen when I approached True, and I had my lil' sister to take care of 'cuz my mama wasn't shit. I don't know why, but I felt bonded to that nigga; no homo. I knew my older sister, Kalila, had been his girl, but I didn't tell him that right away because I didn't want him to put me on because of that. I wanted to prove myself to him, and I did for a whole year.

By the time I was eighteen, I was True's right-hand man since Halo decided to hand everything over to True. All the Chicago Hittas had gone on to do whatever they wanted to do. Bread and Butta took off to NC with their families. Halo was sitting out in Romeoville raising her daughter. It was just me, Kaliyah, True, and Honesty. I met Royalty, and we hit it off. I didn't introduce her to everybody right away.

When my sorry ass mama told me that Halo and I were related, I coulda beat her ass! This whole fucking time I been around my kinfolk and didn't even know it. Once I sat back and really looked at it, we shared a lot of similar features. I was trying to figure out how I missed that shit. I came clean to True, and he put us together. The rest was history. Halo and I were good. I was getting ready to propose to my pregnant girl, and life was good.

True went through some shit with Honesty, but I was glad to see my nigga happy and shit. He even had a daughter, found his birth mom, and found out that he had a lil' sister and brother. Not too long after that, Mama Jayla passed away, and imagine all of our surprises when Kalila showed her funky ass up at the funeral. The whole time her ass had faked her death and was an FBI agent. Shortly after she showed up, her death was displayed all across CNN and all major news stations. She was killed by the Sinaloa Cartel. Shit was brutal.

I proposed to my girl, and she accepted. A nigga was about to have a son and everything. As we speak, I'm waiting on Royalty to drop that load. My son was a week overdue, and her fuck ass doctor didn't want to induce her yet. I was about ten seconds off his ass. Royalty stopped me from fucking his ass up at her last appointment but seeing her in pain made me want to go back on my word.

Everything was running smoothly, and I was completely legit. I bought True's club, Soddom, and Gommorah. Yeah, it was a strip club, but Royalty wasn't worried about that shit. Besides, none of them hoes could amount to my baby. They tried it but got shut down every time. I was a young, rich ass nigga. I knew I looked good, but the thing was, these hoes didn't move me like that. I had a whole ass wife at home. She was the baddest of the baddest to me. These bitches out here couldn't even begin to compete with her.

I was sitting in my office watching Aquafina do her thing. Every time she came in, she brought me a shitload of money. Thirsty ass niggas came from everywhere to see her. She was about her bag, and that was it. She was one of the only ones who came in, did her shit, and went home. I watched the monitors as she hypnotized some nigga with gold fronts at the foot of the stage. He leaned forward and put his whole face into her pussy.

*"Duke, come back."* I radioed.

*"Yeah, Boss?"*

*"Back that nigga off Aquafina's pussy. He gotta pay to touch, sniff, or anything else."*

*"Copy that, Boss."*

I stared intently at the monitors as Duke stalked over to the edge of the stage. He snatched homeboy back by his collar, and I was satisfied. However, Aquafina was not. She looked up, knowing where the cameras were at. A scowl was etched across her face. She slick gave me the middle finger, and I laughed as I went to sit back down in my chair. Just because I said a bitch couldn't compare to my baby didn't mean I wasn't a nigga.

Aquafina finished her set, scooped up her money, and went to the locker room I had for the ladies. I watched her as she stuffed everything in her locker, showered, and redressed. She stomped angrily out the locker room and up the hallway to the elevator. I saw her mash the elevator button repeatedly before it finally came down. She stepped in and pressed the button to the third floor where the private offices were. In no time, she was upstairs and at my office door. She knocked.

"Yo!"

"What the fuck, Savage?" Aquafina asked, storming in.

"What you mean?" I feigned ignorance.

"You always startin' some shit that stops me from gettin' my coins. I'm tired of the fuck shit," she said, crossing her arms over her chest. It just made her titties sit up perfectly.

"Fuck allat! What I tell you?" I said, glaring at her.

"Fuck you, Savage!" she spat.

"You don't mean that, bae," I said, coming from behind my desk.

I grabbed her roughly and pulled her into my body. She melted into my arms instantly. I put my face into her neck and kissed her neck softly. She moaned, and my dick got hard. I shoved her towards my desk, and she quickly assumed the position. I hiked her dress up over her hips, slid a condom over my dick, and plunged into her.

"Uggghhhh!" I moaned. "Fuck I tell you, Jay!" I roared, calling her by her real name.

"Oh, shitttt! Savage, you my baby. This all your pussy," Jay said, throwing her ass back at me.

I caught all the shit she was throwing and busted a satisfying nut. I grunted after releasing my nut into the condom. I mighta been cheating, but I wasn't stupid. Nobody was having my babies but Royalty. I snatched my dick outta Jay and pulled the condom with it. I wasn't taking any chances. I walked to the bathroom and flushed the condom down the toilet. I washed my dick in the sink as Jay laid across my desk.

What? Oh, you thought because I said I had a badass wife at home that I wasn't being a nigga? Shittttt! I was still young as fuck, and even though Royalty was everything a nigga needed and more, I still wanted to sample other shit from time to time. Jay was the only bitch who wasn't pressed over a nigga. She kept her mouth shut, and the rest of these hoes didn't even know I was sticking dick to her. She was low-key as fuck, and that's what I wanted. Jay wasn't worth my wife in no damn way, and she knew that. This just worked for us.

I walked out the bathroom to see Jay was still sprawled across my desk. I smacked her on the ass, and she fell over. What the fuck? I shook the shit out of her but got no response. I checked her for a pulse and everything but couldn't find one. I smacked her hard as fuck in her face, and she didn't move. Oh, fuck! Oh, shit! Oh, fuck! I grabbed my radio and called Duke. Ten minutes later, he walked in my office and saw her laying on the floor.

"What happened, Boss?"

"Shit, the usual, but when I came out the bathroom, she hadn't moved yet. When I touched her, she fell over. I think she's dead, fam. I saw enough dead bodies to know that shit."

"You fucked her to death?" Duke choked out a laugh.

Even though that shit was funny, this was no laughing manner. I had to figure out a way to get this bitch out my office and still get my ass home on time. Just as I was about to call somebody to scoop this broad up, Royalty called. I answered as calm as possible.

*"Hey bae, you good?"*

*"It's time, baby. Mama is taking me to Mercy. Meet*

*us there."*

*"On my way. I love you."*

FUCK! I put in the call and let Duke know not to let anyone in my office until Scottie got there. He gave me a head nod, and I was out the door. I stopped Dank and let him know he was in charge until Duke got back on the floor. I took off out the door, hopped in my whip, and hit the e-way. My son was on the way!

# CHAPTER TWO

## ROYALTY

My mama was with me at our condo when my water broke. For the last three weeks, she'd been there with me, Kavion and Kaliyah. She was such a Godsend because I didn't wanna do shit but have this damn baby. I almost had to stop Kavion from killing my doctor last week. With Kavion buying True's club, it made me happy that he wasn't running the streets anymore. That shit was scary enough, but at least with a club, I knew he wasn't taking a risk of getting killed. I was glad he was back to being plain ole Kavion. I didn't like calling him Savage anyway unless we were having sex, and that's how I ended up pregnant anyway.

I huffed and puffed as I waddled down the hallway. I told my mama to get the car ready and have it near the elevator. We bought this condo because I loved the city. It was right on Lake Shore Drive. Mostly, we stayed at our home in Elgin, but when we came to the city and were too tired to go home, we stayed here. I was having the baby at Mercy Hospital, so we'd been staying close.

Kaliyah grabbed my bag and locked up behind me. We stepped on the elevator together, and as soon as the doors opened, my mama was waiting with the door open. I slid in the seat slowly, breathing hard as shit. I felt nothing but pressure, and I screamed out.

"Hold on, sis. Your contractions are a minute-and-a-half apart. Mama, speed all the way to the hospital. If the cops get behind us, let them," Kaliyah said, trying to soothe me.

"Hush, girl. I know what I'm doing. Make sure y'all buckle up. I already called the police and let them know what kinda car I'm driving and what the situation is. A squad car is supposed to be downstairs waiting on us."

"Just drive, damn it!" I yelled out.

My mama did just that. When we got downstairs, she stopped briefly to let the officer get in front of us with his lights on. We sped all the way to Mercy, and as soon as I walked in, they had a gurney waiting for me. As I laid down on the bed, Kavion came crashing through the doors. He took my hand and kissed my face. I didn't miss the smell of perfume on him, but I'd address it after I got this big-headed baby out of me.

They wheeled me up to labor and delivery. I was barely in the room for fifteen minutes when I felt like I had to push. I told the nurse, and she tried to calm me down saying since it was my first baby, I had plenty of time. I guess Kavion didn't like that shit.

"Look here, bitch, either you get the doctor, or I'ma

have to get the coroner in this bitch. My wife said she felt like she had to push. She knows her body better than you do. Get the fuckin' doctor now!" He barked.

That nurse ran up outta my room like her ass was on fire! Not even five seconds later, a doctor was storming into the room. She quickly washed her hands and put on some latex gloves. She pulled my blanket back and immediately screeched.

"Oh, boy! Looks like baby said it's time to come now. Give me a push on your next contraction, hun."

Kavion glared at the nurse standing to the right of the doctor. I knew he wanted to wring her damn neck, or even worse, kill her for doubting me. I felt the next contraction, so I squeezed his hand as I pushed. I gritted my teeth and pushed with all my might. I felt a small sense of relief but then another contraction hit me, so I pushed again. I pushed two more times before my son's cries filled the room. I fell back to the bed exhausted.

I watched as the nurses cleaned up my baby with Kavion watching them like a hawk. I pushed out the afterbirth, and the doctor cleaned me up. I was tired as hell. Childbirth was no damn joke, but I'd do it all over again. I was happy to become a mom. The nurse swaddled my son and brought him over to me. When she placed him in my arms, it was like all my emotions hit me at once. I started crying as I held him.

"Bae, he's so beautiful. Look at all his hair. Oh, my gosh! Thank you, bae. Thank you so fuckin' much. I love you."

All I could do was cry because my son was the most beautiful thing ever. He had a head full of hair. His caramel colored skin was so soft. His eyes were closed, and his tiny hand was wrapped around my finger. Another cry escaped his lips, and that's when the nurse told me to try to feed him. I pulled my gown back and put my breast to my son's mouth. He greedily latched on and sucked. His little hands gripped each side of my breast as he ate. I was just in awe.

"You're going to want to try to feed him at least every two to three hours. Skin to skin contact is best also. I'll take him to the nursery in about two hours to get his first tests and shots out the way. Enjoy your baby boy," a nurse told us walking away.

Once everyone cleared the room, it was just me, Kavion, and our son. I was still shocked that this little human came from me. I would love him till the death of me. I placed him in Kavion's arms as he sat next to me after I burped him. I was tired as hell, but my mind wouldn't let my body rest worth a damn. Just as I was about to question my husband about why he smelled like another woman, my mama came busting into the room.

"Lemme see my grandbaby. Give 'em here, Kavion," she said eagerly.

Kavion slid the baby into her arms, and she started to coo at him. She sat down in the chair and talked to our son like he understood what the hell she was saying. I asked Kavion to help me to the bathroom. He did and waited patiently as I used it. I washed my hands, and he guided me back to bed carefully helping me in. I got settled and was just about to doze off when I heard commotion out in the hallway. All the noise scared my son, and Kavion went to find out what the hell was going on.

"Fuck that shit y'all talkin'! That's my grandson, and I want to see him. I have the right to see him! Move the fuck outta my way," I heard Kavion's mama yelling in the hallway once he opened the door.

He ran out in the hallway to stop whatever rampage she was on. We both had agreed that his mama would have nothing to do with our son. There was no way in hell we'd ever be comfortable with a crack head around our child, let alone in our lives. That was a no go for me for sure. I strained to get up, but my mama placed my son in his bassinet, rolled it over to me, and pushed me back in the bed.

"This old bitch got me fucked up! I keep telling folks

I'm saved, but they wanna test my gangsta. Lord forgive me for whooping this bitch's ass up in this hospital. At least she won't have to go far to get to the emergency room."

"Mama!" I shrieked. "Mama, please don't do nothin'."

"Nah, fuck that! When she popped up the first damn time I didn't like her ass. I still don't like that bald-headed hoe. Ain't never did shit for Kavion or Kaliyah but think she has rights to my grandson? I think the fuck not! If she had edges still I'd snatch them shits off her ass!"

"Mama, stop!" I said snickering.

"Tell her ugly ass to stop. Why is she even here? Out in the damn hallway acting an ass looking like a fucked-up Rainbow Brite on that shit. What she gon' do for my grandbaby besides try to steal his formula and sell it for a rock? Not on my damn watch. Fuck outta here!"

I was dying laughing at my mama. My stomach already hurt, but laughing made it worse. She was dead ass serious, and I knew she didn't play any games when it came to me, so it would be the same way with my baby. She didn't even play when it came to Kavion or Kaliyah because she loved them that much. He had told her what his mama did when they were younger so, because I loved him and his sister, she did too. She was on good bullshit right now.

She rolled her sleeves up, hiked up her skirt, and

headed towards the door. I couldn't just hop outta bed and go after her, so I said to hell with it. Served her ass right if you asked me. I heard my mama yelling and then Ms. Faulks started screaming.

"Yousa sorry ass, crack head ass, two-dollar ass hoe. Up here causing problems for my chirren like you give a fuck 'bout them. I told myself I was saved, but you need this sanctified ass whooping I'm giving you, bitch. Now, go the fuck on before ya' son gotta bury ya' ass. Lordt! Please forgive me for the sins I just committed. Amen."

I was laughing so hard at my mama that I didn't even notice the police come on the floor. I struggled as best as I could to get out the bed and hobble to the door. When I got into the hallway, they were putting my mama in handcuffs, and Ms. Faulks was laid out on the hallway floor. I stifled a laugh and started pleading to the police.

"Please officers, don't take my mama to jail. She was just defending me. That lady," I said pointing at Ms. Faulks, "came into my room and tried to snatch me off my bed after having my baby. She's a drug-addict, and she's mad that her son and I don't want her around our newborn."

The officer who had my mama in cuffs looked at Kavion who corroborated my story. That seemed to really set Ms. Faulks off because she was no longer laying on the ground playing like my mama had knocked her out.

"That bitch a bald-faced ass lie. That's my grandbaby, and I was defending him and my daughter. She means them no good, and I'd be remiss as a mother if I didn't protect what was mine."

After a few hushed conversations, my mama was released from the cuffs. She headed straight to me and got me back into bed. I left Kavion to deal with the mess in the hallway. Now that I was sure that Ms. Faulks was no longer a threat, I relaxed and went to sleep. When I woke up, only Kavion was in the room, and my son was not. I stretched and felt my breasts start to ache. Before I called the nurse, I needed to talk to my husband.

"Kavion! Wake the fuck up! We need to talk!" I said yelling at him.

"Damn bae, what's wrong?"

"I wanna know why the fuck you smelled like another woman earlier? All the time we've been together and even the small amount of time you've been owning the club, you never came home smelling like another woman. What the fuck is really going on, Kavion and don't lie to me?" I seethed.

Kavion brushed his hand down his face before he got up from the recliner and came to me.

"Remember that new bitch Aquafina at the club that I

hired? Well, she came on to me saying we could fuck and dassit, but I wasn't going. She pushed up on me, and I had to call Duke to escort her ass up outta there. I fired that hoe on the spot. Everybody knows I have a wife that I love more than life. I would NEVER disrespect you ever in both of our lives. She ain't shit, bae, and you ain't got nothin' to worry about."

I searched for the lie in his face, but I found none. I was pacified for the time being, but if I ever found out that my husband lied, that was his ass. I called the nurse for my baby, fed and burped him, and went back to sleep. Visions of my son and my family danced in my head.

# CHAPTER THREE

## SAVAGE

That was a close ass call. After Mama James showed out and whooped my mama's ass, I had to deal with Royalty's hormonal ass asking me about another bitch. I didn't even realize that I smelled like Aquafina's ass, but I had my explanation ready. All my girls at the club knew who my wife was. They didn't compare in any way at all, so explaining the shit with Aquafina was easy.

Once I got Royalty settled into bed for the night, I snuck away to call Duke to make sure that shit was handled. Mama James decided to stay with Royalty, so I took that opportunity to handle my business.

*"Yeah, Boss?"* Duke said, answering his phone.

*"Is that situation handled?"*

*"Scottie came twenty minutes after you left. Situation resolved, Boss. How's the baby?"*

*"Royalty and my son are good. A nigga happy as hell right now."*

*"Good shit. You deserve it. I got you till you come back, Boss."*

*"Aye man, cut it out with all the boss shit. We been friends how long, Duke? We more than friends, we family."*

*"Roger that. Just do what you gotta do, and I got it over here."*

*"I appreciate you, Duke, and when I get back to the office, take ya' girl somewhere nice."*

I hung up the phone, and my next call was to True. I had to let him know that his nephew was born. Nigga was clear across the country right now. His ass better watch out. As light-skinned, as he is,was with his good ass hair, muthafuckas might mistake his ass for a Mexican and deport his ass. Y'all know Trump on some bullshit about this wall and border security.

*"My nigga, what's good?"* True said, answering the phone.

*"My bad for hitting you up so late, but my son is here. You an uncle, my nigga."*

*"That's what the fuck is up! What y'all name him?"*

*"Sir True Faulk,"* I answered proudly.

*"Dead ass? You named the lil' nigga after me?"*

*"You my brother, so why wouldn't I? I never got a chance to say this, but I appreciate you for everything you've ever done for me. Every opportunity you've given me has brought more to me than I'd ever seen in my life. For that, I'm grateful. It was only right to give my son your name."*

*"Look here, lil' nigga, you 'bout to make a thug shed*

*real tears," True said, sharing a laugh with me. "I'll fly in
this weekend with the family to see him. Honesty gon' be
happy as shit."*

I hung up my phone, checked a few emails, and
responded to a text or two before heading back into my
wife's room. When I walked in, she was just reaching for our
son.

"I got him, bae. Get some rest."

She didn't even bother to respond, she just climbed
back into bed. I fed my son as he sucked greedily from the
small formula bottle. Once he was finished, I placed him over
my shoulder to burp him. After he burped, I just held him in
my arms and admired him. It was one of the most surrealist
things in the world. I was a father! Shit felt so damn good,
and I couldn't wait to give my son a brother or sister. Royalty
would probably kick my ass for even thinking about that
right now.

I called the nurse to take my son to the nursery for a
few hours so Royalty could sleep. I needed to get to the crib
and shower, grab us some clothes, and handle a few things
before I came back. Today was inventory day at the club, and
I needed to make sure that shit ran smooth. The manager,
Dyonna, was thorough, but I still liked checking my own
shit. I quickly showered and dressed, grabbed our shit, and
left. I headed straight back to the hospital.

***

When I got back, Royalty and Mama James were still asleep. I peeked in on them before heading to the nursery to see my son. I got to the window and looked in at him. He was so perfect. I still couldn't believe I was a father. It hit me like a ton of bricks. I was gon' give my son the fuckin' world. Him and my wife were everything. I prayed that I could keep my urges to myself from now on. I knew that me and Royalty were young when we got together, but I knew she was the woman I wanted for life. I had to wife her up, even if I did dumb shit. She was my everything.

Ten plus years is a long time to be with someone. I loved Royalty with every part of me, but I got with her when I was eighteen. We didn't get married until I popped the question on her birthday not that long ago. When she said yes, we didn't even plan a wedding. We headed straight down to City Hall and got married. We threw a small party with just our family. With her being close to having the baby before this, I was feeling a little overwhelmed. I slipped up here and there, but Aquafina, aka Jay, was the one I had been messing with the longest.

I had all this money at such a young age, and I really wasn't flashy. Shit, I still had the Bentley that True bought me for my eighteenth birthday. I had my shit together on the home front, and my business was in order. It was just the fact that money brought hoes, and it brought 'em in abundance. Bitches knew what it was when they would fuck with me. Outside of Royalty, I never met family, went on outings, or any of that extra shit; except when I met Jay. Jay made a nigga do different shit.

I met her mama and sister. I had been spending bread on her and shit. I was even taking her out to low-key spots just to spend time with her. A nigga caught feelings; I ain't even gon' lie. She was my top money maker at the club too! I didn't mind her dancing and shit because she wasn't my main bitch, but I still felt some kind of way when niggas paid her too much attention. Since I gave a fuck about Jay like that, I told the fellas not to make her disappear. Her people deserved to be able to bury her the right way.

I left the hospital after making sure my family was good and headed to the club. Pulling into the parking lot, I saw Dyonna's car. I also saw another car that I recognized. When I parked and got out, the door flew open on the small Ford Focus that was parked on the other side of Dyonna's. Jay's mama, Lana, climbed out and headed in my direction.

"Savage! Have you seen Jay? She didn't come home last night, and I've been calling her, but it's going straight to voicemail. I'm worried."

"She left here about two and said she was stopping to

get something to eat before going home. She never even texted me to say she made it. I didn't pay it no mind though because she doesn't always text me to let me know she made it safe," I said shrugging.

"Aren't you worried about your woman? What kinda man are you?"

"The kind that's married, and all y'all know that. What me and Jay have works for us, but she knows I'm married. So do you and Tisha. Do I care about her? Yeah, but not enough to worry about her over my wife and family. I don't know what to tell you, but don't bring no shit to my club. Go find Jay and leave me the hell alone." I snapped, walking off.

"So help me God, if something happened to my daughter, I know it's your fault. I'll be back, asshole."

I waved her ass off not paying her no mind. I was good with my shit, and I spoke nothing but the truth to Lana. She was cappin' for no damn reason. I walked inside the club leaving her outside glaring at me. Dyonna was standing near the bar with an iPad. I walked over to her for an update.

"What's good? All the deliveries come yet?"

"So far, the domestic beer delivery came; so has the top-shelf liquor and Pepsi. I'm waiting for the food delivery, and then I can check everything in. I forwarded six emails to you about patrons wanting to use the club for their parties or gatherings. Everything is good, Boss."

"Appreciate your work ethic, Dyonna. Aye, you saw that lady out in the parking lot? She say anything to you?"

"When I pulled up, she was there. She asked me where you were, and I told her I had no clue because I just work here."

"If you see her again, don't let her in here. That's Aquafina's mama. Apparently, Aquafina didn't come home last night, so she thinks I know something, and she might cause drama at my club. I don't need no bad business."

"Well, maybe Aquafina will show up later. She's a grown ass woman. What she does when she leaves here is none of our business. Her mama got a lot of nerve thinking you know where your employees go when they leave here."

She didn't even know the half of it. I was discreet as fuck when I started dealing with Jay. Nobody in my club but Duke knew that we had a thing going on. There was no paper trail. I made sure that whatever I did with her was kept on the down low. I didn't need shit to get back to my wife and make her leave me. Royalty was everything to me, and even though I was being a dumb ass nigga, I didn't want to lose her.

I headed to my office and sat down at my big, oak desk. I logged in and checked my emails that Dyonna sent me. I replied to four of the six emails. The other two were straight trash. I didn't do bullshit in my club. I didn't give a fuck who it was, and these dumb niggas had the audacity to pretty much say they wanted me to let them in the club fully-armed. Not on my damn watch. Last thing I needed was a shootout in my shit.

I called Mama James to check in on Royalty and Sir. I heard his little cry in the background, and it pulled at my heart. She let me know they were good, and I let her know I'd be there shortly. I called in an order for some tacos and shit for Mama James and Royalty. I shot a text to Duke and then headed back to the hospital picking the food up on the way. When I parked in the garage, my phone went off.

**Duke: Aquafina's body was just found....check out the news**

I headed inside, got to the room, and gave the food to Mama James and Royalty. As they devoured their food, I turned the news on. Sure as shit, there was a breaking news banner running across the bottom of the screen. I turned it up to see what they were saying. Scottie was creative as fuck this time. I'd have to send him a lil' extra for pulling this shit off the way he did.

*"Early this morning, the body and car of a woman was found near the city's west side. From the looks of it, it appears that the woman went into distress, and her car*

*crashed head on to this light pole you see behind us. Sources are saying the young woman went into cardiac arrest while driving home from work. She's been identified as twenty-four-year-old Jayonna Morales, an exotic dancer at Soddom and Gommorah night club. Her family has already been notified."*

"Damn! That's some fucked up shit. She was young as hell. How the hell did she have a heart attack? Did she use drugs or something?" Royalty asked out loud.

"I'ont know. As far as I know, she didn't. I don't allow anyone to work for me who indulges in drugs. It takes away from the fantasy that they're supposed to create for the people who come to the club. Can't look attractive and alluring if ya' ass is twitchin'.'"

Royalty didn't say anything else and went back to eating. Mama James was killing her burrito plate and didn't even chime in. I washed my hands and took off my hoodie before picking my son up. Lil' nigga didn't even wake up. He stretched a lil' bit, but that was it. I sat down on the edge of the bed and looked at my wife.

"You know that as soon as the doctor clears you, I'm knocking you up again, right? I need a lil' you now. That would make us complete."

"Boy, you do see me sitting here right? How the hell you gon' tell my daughter you knockin' her up again in my presence? Lord, let us pray for this child. He up here talkin' 'bout what he's gonna do with his penis in front of his elder. Forgive him, Father," Mama James said with her eyes closed.

This lady was a trip, but I loved her. She definitely kept me on my toes as much as her daughter did. I wouldn't trade none of this shit for the world. I just hoped that this shit with Aquafina didn't come back to bite me in the ass.

# CHAPTER FOUR

## LANA

I went to confront Savage, but he claimed to not know where my daughter was. When I got home, the police were sitting outside my home. My heart jumped out of my chest when they approached me and asked me about Jayonna. They told me that her car had crashed due to the fact that she had a heart attack. My daughter was a happy and healthy twenty-four-year-old. There's no way in hell she had a damn heart attack.

"I need to see my baby. Where is she? Take me to my baby!" I shouted.

"Ma'am, we understand you're in pain right now. Is there someone who can drive you down to the coroner's office? It wouldn't be a good idea for you to go alone."

"Yes, my other daughter. I'll call her right now. Just tell me where I need to go."

The cop rattled off the address as I dialed Tisha's number. I could barely tell her that her big sister was dead. The cop took my phone from me and explained to Tisha what was going on. He gave her the address again and hung up. He led me over to my car and opened the door so I could sit down. I felt like I was hyperventilating. I couldn't breathe, and my chest felt tight as hell.

"Ma'am, are you ok? Should I call an ambulance for you?" the cop asked concerned.

"No," I choked out. "I just need my inhaler," I said, reaching for my purse.

The cop took my purse and rummaged through it for my inhaler. Just as she handed it to me, a car swooped into the driveway. I saw Tisha hop out and run over to me.

"Mommy, is this for real? Jay's really gone?" she asked with tears in her eyes.

I just shook my head yes. For the longest time, it was just us three. Their father left me when Tisha was four and never came back. Now I had to bury my baby. I didn't give a fuck what that nigga Savage said. I knew he had something to do with my daughter's death, and I was gonna prove it. Tisha pulled me out my car and locked it before leading me to her car. I slid into the passenger seat while she held the door open. My chest still hurt.

Once she got in the car, we headed straight to Cook County Coroner's Office. When we got in front, my feet felt like cement bricks. I started hyperventilating again and had to use my inhaler once more. Tisha ran over to my side of the car and gripped me in a tight hug.

"We gon' get through this together, Mama. Let's go take care of this." Tisha cried into my ear.

I clung to my only and remaining child as we walked up the steps into the building. I stopped at the receptionist desk to let them know who I was and what I was there to do. The lady directed me to the elevators where I had to go down one floor and check in with that receptionist there. This was by far one of the hardest things I'd ever have to do in my life. A mother should never bury her child. I checked in, and she pointed down the long, lonely looking hallway.

With each step that I took, my heart broke a little more. This was my first-born. Part of my heart. The reason that I lived and breathed. We got to a set of double doors that had a clear, glass window to the right of them. We saw a body covered by a sheet laying on the metal table. I pushed through the doors and out of nowhere, a man appeared.

"May I help you?"

"Yes. I'm here to identify my daughter's body. She was in a car accident after having a heart attack at the wheel. At least that's what the police told me."

"Yes, ma'am. What is the deceased person's name?"

"Jayonna Morales."

He checked his clipboard and nodded his head.

"Follow me please."

"Wait, this isn't her?" I asked, pointing to the covered

body.

"No, ma'am. She's just in the next room."

Tisha and I followed behind him. We were in another room just like the previous one, and another body lay atop a metal slab with a sheet covering it. I walked over to the table, and he pulled the sheet down just enough to show her face. As soon as I saw Jay's face, my knees went weak, but Tisha caught me. I let out a loud yell and felt my body temperature rise. Everything faded to black around me.

***

When I woke up, I noticed I was in a hospital bed. Tisha was asleep in the chair next to me. An oxygen mask was over my face, and I felt light-headed. I sat up, and I felt like something had hit me really hard over the head. I hurried to sit back and took a deep breath. Everything felt groggy, and my throat was dry as hell.

"Tisha." I croaked out.

"Oh, my gosh, Mommy, are you ok?"

"No. My mind is all foggy. What happened?"

"You passed out when we went to identify Jay's body."

"So, it's real? She's really dead?" I asked, that dread creeping back into my heart.

"Yes, Mommy," Tisha replied with tears in her eyes.

I clutched my chest. This was too much. I had to plan for a funeral that I was hoping wasn't for real. Jayonna was one-third of my heart. She was one of the reasons I lived and worked so hard. Even without their father helping me, I made a decent living as a registered nurse. Tears dripped down my face as Tisha hugged me. I had a fleeting thought.

"An autopsy. I forgot to request an autopsy," I said panicked.

"Relax, Mommy. I already told him we wanted one done. I don't believe that Jay had a heart attack any more than I believe that she crashed her car into a pole."

I relaxed a little knowing that Tisha handled what I couldn't. I felt it in my heart that Savage had everything to do with my daughter's death. Now I just had to prove it. How the fuck would I do that?

# CHAPTER FIVE

## JAYONNA

*I guess this is me speaking from the grave. I never thought I'd end up dead at twenty-four. I had my shit all mapped out for me. I was a beautiful ass woman. I had curves for days with a pretty face to match. I always knew that my beauty would get me places that my intellect wouldn't. I was smart as a whip, but unfortunately for me, men couldn't see past my shape. I was a threat to most women because not only was I pretty, I was smart as fuck too!*

*When I started working at S & D, it was for the sole purpose of paying for school. Typical stripper shit, except I didn't do what typical strippers did. While they were fucking for extra dollars, niggas were paying me for pure fantasy. I never had to suck or ride a dick to get my coins. All I had to do was dance for a nigga seductively enough to make him come out his pockets. I'd been propositioned by many a man to become his lil' side piece for a large amount of money. I wasn't one of those bitches that could be bought though.*

*How I started dealing with Savage was something that came out of left field. He exuded power, and his presence alone demanded respect. I noticed that the other dancers talked about wanting to fuck him six ways from Sunday, but he only had eyes for his wife. I took that shit as a personal challenge because not only did he have the money, but he had the connections to get me where I wanted to be. Ultimately, I wanted to be a physician's assistant with my own clinic. Fucking with Savage was gonna get me what I needed.*

*I fucked around and caught feelings for the nigga even knowing he had a wife. He fucked me good, and the cash was amazing! He even met my family. Even though I was dealt the side chick role, I played my part. Nobody even knew that we were fucking around. He tossed bands at me here and there, and them shits went straight to my bank account. I knew I caught feelings when one day I went to his office and his wife, his very pregnant wife, was in there. I played it off like I had a question about a set I wanted to do and left.*

*I went straight home after that not even wanting to work that night knowing she was in the building. I got a call from a nigga who wanted to spend major bread for a dancer, and I accepted. I showed up at the Trump Hotel and did my thing. I partied with the white boy whose party it was, and next thing you know, I was snorting my first line. That night I was on a high like nothing I'd ever felt before. Soon after, I found myself doing lines of coke to keep my feelings out the way when it came to Savage.*

*My addiction to coke got outta hand, and I realized that I was doing side jobs just to take care of my addiction. I still had a goal in mind and swore myself to rehab once I got the money I needed to start my clinic up. When I did my set the night I died, I had been on a coke binge all day. All that extra shit pumping through my body plus liquor and the adrenaline rush I got from the sex was just too much for my heart.*

*I remember feeling Savage pull his dick from me while I laid across his desk. I couldn't speak or scream out or nothing. All I could do was lay there. As I faded into darkness, all I could think about was my mom and little sister. Please forgive me y'all. I did the one thing I told myself I would never let happen. I allowed a man to get the best of me so much so to the point that I ended up ruining my life. Talk about fucked up.*

# CHAPTER SIX

## ROYALTY

Something in my spirit would just not let me believe my husband. I was skeptical to talk to my mama about it because all she was gonna say was if I thought something was wrong, then it probably was. I'd been with this man for a decade. I'd been everything his ass needed me to be. If I found out some foul shit, me and my baby were gone. You hear me? GONE! I wouldn't settle for no shit like that when we got together, and I damn sure wouldn't settle for it now.

I decided that once I went for this one-week check-up, I was gonna stop at Kavion's club. My appointment was in four days. I was gonna put my best shit on and show the fuck out if I found anything out of the ordinary. Those four little days flew by, and as Kavion and I sat in the doctor's office with Sir, some chick was staring a hole through his head. I found that shit suspect as hell.

I waited until we got into a room in the back of the office to question my husband who seemed oblivious to the bitch in the waiting room. I took Sir's blanket off him and made sure he was comfortable before turning to my husband.

"Kavion, you got something you wanna tell me?"

"Nah bae, why you ask me that?"

"'Cuz it was a bitch in the waiting room mugging the shit outta you. Women don't just go around doing shit like that for no reason."

"I'on know that bitch. I'on know why she was staring either. Maybe she's just jealous of you 'cuz her nigga wasn't in the waiting room with her like yours was."

"Yeah, ok. Let me find the fuck out, Kavion. I already told you when we got together, don't play with my heart. I will fuck yo' ass up!" I spat at him.

He looked completely unbothered by what I had just said, so it made me think I was overreacting. Still, my gut was telling me I was on to something. The doctor came in and checked both me and Sir out. We were given a clean bill of health and sent on our way. I made a six-week appointment for us and walked out behind Kavion to our car. As I was getting ready to slide my ass in my seat, the same woman from the waiting room approached our car. I hopped out with the quickness. Last thing I needed was some crazy bitch to do something to my baby.

"Does your wife know about my sister?" the woman asked.

"Kavion, what is she talking about?"

"Oh, Kavion, huh? Couldn't even tell my sister your real name. That's a damn shame."

"Look, back the fuck up outta my face with that bullshit. I'on know who the fuck you are, nor do I know your damn sister. Get the fuck on!"

"Babe, what the fuck?"

"Just get in the car and don't listen to what this crazy bitch is talkin' 'bout. I don't fuckin' know her!"

I headed back to my side of the car to get in because I was gonna say what I needed to say on the drive home. As soon as I got ready to close my door, 'ol girl screamed at my husband.

"Now you wanna act like you don't know my sister because you're with your bougie-ass wife? Fuck her and fuck you too! I told Jay about fucking with you, but she wouldn't listen. Now she's dead, and I know you had something to do with that shit. I'ma make sure ya' ass gets put under the fucking jail. On God!"

"Who's your sister?" I asked.

She turned her attention to me. "She was a dancer at his club. Her name is Jay, but her stage name was Aquafina."

I closed my door and didn't say another word. I saw the hurt in her eyes. I saw the recognition flash over Kavion's face. I knew he knew the girl she was talking about. It was the same dancer we just watched the news report about after I had our son. Kavion got in the car and looked in my direction.

"Look, bae, I can explain."

"Save that shit, Kavion. I told you a long time ago to not hurt me. I made that crystal clear to you. Now I find out about some shit like this, and of all places, in front of my doctor's office. I just have one damn question. How long was it going on?"

He dropped his head and sighed before answering me. I didn't wanna cry, but I couldn't help the tears falling from my eyes as he told me what he had going on with this woman. All types of shit was running through my head. Was I not pretty enough? Good enough? Was I fucking him the wrong way? Not cooking enough? Then I had to realize, it wasn't my fault. He was being a nigga. Well, that nigga just lost his wife.

"Drive me the fuck home, Kavion, and don't say shit else to me."

I couldn't believe this man. I didn't even know who he was anymore. There was no way I was about to accept any of this shit. I pulled my phone from my purse and booked a room for myself and my son. Kavion needed to see that this shit was serious, and I wouldn't stand for it. This was more than cheating with some thot ass stripper. This was about loyalty, trust, and honesty. Ten years I'd given this man. Ten fuckin' years! And he goes and does some shit like this. Nah,

I can't deal.

When we got home, I headed straight to our bedroom. I grabbed my rolling suitcase and duffle bag and placed it on the bed before removing my clothes from the dresser. I literally packed all the shit I knew I wanted and said fuck the rest. I went into the bathroom and grabbed my personal hygiene items. I double-checked to make sure I had everything I wanted before grabbing my suitcase, duffle bag, and purse and headed back outside.

I tossed everything in the third-row seat of my Armada and went back inside to get my son. Kavion had me fucked up. I snatched up the car seat and went to go find that nigga and my son. He was sitting in Sir's room rocking him in the rocking chair.

"Give me my son so I can go. I don't have time for the games you playin'."

"You can go. My son isn't going anywhere."

"Like hell. Stop playing this bullshit ass game with me, Kavion, and give me my child."

"He's my son too!" Kavion yelled.

Sir started crying, and I reached for him, but Kavion pushed me back. He turned his back and laid Sir in his crib while he screamed at the top of his lungs. He pushed me up against the wall and held me there tightly.

"I fucked up, alright? I know I fucked up but lemme

make it right. Don't leave me, Royalty. Please, don't leave me."

"You shoulda thought about that shit when you started fucking somebody else. Did you think I would just overlook that shit and we'd live happily ever after? I gave you all of me, and you gave another woman what was supposed to be only mine! You gave away half of you to a woman that wasn't even half of me. Fuck you, Kavion. Let me the fuck go!"

I pushed him off of me, and he let me go. I picked my son up and walked out his room. As I placed my son in his car seat, tears streamed down my face. My heart was broken. I didn't know if I could get over this type of betrayal. All I knew was that I needed to get away from him right now before I used his own gun on him. I got my son situated, and we left. I strapped Sir into the back seat and rolled out.

I pulled my phone out and hooked it to the Bluetooth speaker so I could call my mama. She answered right away.

*"Mama, I need you," I said crying.*

*"Come home, baby."*

*"No! He'll just come there. I got a room. Meet me there."*

*"Send me the information, and I'm on my way."*

When I stopped at the light, I texted my mama the

hotel info. This was gonna be a long road to travel, and I was just glad I had my mama to travel it with me.

# CHAPTER SEVEN

## MAMA JAMES

Normally I wouldn't get mixed up in Royalty's life like that, but this wasn't just anything. Kavion was her husband, so I needed to have my daughter's back. I could understand her heartbreak and pain. I was in love with her daddy a long time ago. I was also a good girl just like her, but he broke my heart. He didn't just break my heart, but he did that shit with my cousin. Royalty didn't know that she'd been around her daddy all her life, but he never did shit for her. He chose my cousin over me and our daughter. Talk about life fucking you up.

I threw myself into single parenthood and took care of my daughter to the best of my ability. I worked two jobs so Royalty could have everything she needed and then some. I wouldn't ever let her go without. I wasn't always saved, but I tried to keep my faith in God as much as I could. I drove towards the hotel Royalty told me she was staying in with a lot on my mind. I really wanted to drive to their house and beat Kavion's ass because I know he had to have done something to her, but the God in me wouldn't allow that to happen.

Everybody thought I was this sweet, little, old church lady. On the outside, that's exactly what I looked like. On the inside though, I was a Chicago girl to heart. There was fire and ice in my veins. I did whatever was necessary to make sure me and mine were good. A few years back, like way back, when Royalty was about nine, her funky ass daddy showed up on our doorstep. Nigga was really fishing for some shit 'cuz love didn't live here no more for his ass.

He tried to push up on me and got his ass handled. That's why that nigga walked with a limp now. Luckily, Royalty was at school, so she didn't see anything. I didn't play about mine. This man thought he could come to my house, try that slick shit and get back in with me. Na-uh! Not today Satan. After I fucked him up and sent him on his way, my bald-headed ass cousin brought her ass over trying to fight me. She was hollering out all types of shit saying I was trying to steal her man and whatnot. I whooped her ass too! I was tired of people testing my gangsta.

I was well into my sixties now, but I still didn't play those games. I told Kavion when I first met him that he better not hurt my baby. He saw what I did to his damn mama at the hospital. He could try me if he wanted to. I was about to bring my savage out, and it was nothing pretty. Kavion thought I didn't know nothing about his street life. I knew what the streets called him. I was the real savage though.

I parked in the parking garage and headed to the floor Royalty said she was on. I found the room and knocked on her door. I said a silent prayer that this nigga didn't put his hands on my baby or all bets were off. I'd say a prayer for his ass after they find him in the Chicago River. Mama James didn't play about Royalty or Sir. Royalty swung the door open and fell into my arms.

"Oh, baby girl, mama's here. Mama's right here."

Royalty sobbed in my arms as I guided us over to the couch. We sat down, and she became unhinged right in front of me. I felt so bad and wanted to go fuck Kavion up. I let her get it all out before I asked her anything. Her loud sobs subsided, and she looked at me with a tear stained face.

"Mama, I gave Kavion everything. How could he do this to me? To us?"

"Tell me what happened, baby."

"You remember that day at the hospital when we watched the news?"

"You talkin' about that car crash of the girl who worked down at his club?"

"Yeah. That girl's sister approached us today when we were leaving the doctor's office. I saw her in the waiting room first, but he swore he didn't know her."

"Well, you know some women lie. Tell me you talked

to him first before believing what another woman tried to tell you about your husband?"

"He told me everything, Mama. He was spending time and money on that girl. He met her mama and sister. That tells me that he cared for her, and if he cared for her, then there's no way he could truly love me."

"I believe that Kavion loves you. It's just, men are dumb as hell sometimes. Take some time and do what you need to do for yourself and Sir. Mama's got your back."

"Did you ever go through something like this with Daddy?"

"Chile, did I? Your daddy was a real piece of work. Fine thang too, but he was just like all these other dogs out here. Not all men are fucked up individuals, but some of them are. Some of them learn from their mistakes, and some of them continue to be dumb asses. You just gotta figure out what category Kavion fits into. Now ya' know, if you want, I can go cut his ass? It won't hurt me none to do it."

"Mama, no!" Royalty said laughing. "He's still my husband even if I don't like his ass right now."

"I'm just saying. I'll go to war for you and my grandson, and I don't care who it is. Just give me the word, and I'll go handle my business. I'll repent later. God will forgive me because I got it like that with him. We here," I said, motioning back and forth with my hand.

"You're a mess, Mama. I'm glad you're here with me. I love you."

"I love you too, princess. Now, where's my grandson at?"

She pointed to the room, so I went that way. I found Sir sleeping soundly, so I decided not to wake him up. I went to use the bathroom and saw the big, garden-style tub. After I finished and washed my hands, I ran a bath for my baby. She needed to relax and forget about today for right now. I turned the water on and let it run until the tub was full. I went back out to the living room area to tell Royalty to get in the tub, but she had fallen asleep. My poor baby.

I went to drain the tub, and since both my babies were asleep, I decided to step out for a little while. I had a date with a nigga who decided to play with my daughter's emotions. Even though I knew Royalty would be pissed, I had to do what I had to do. I grabbed the keycard and left. I shot a text to Royalty's phone, so she wouldn't worry if she woke up and I wasn't back yet. I called Kavion's phone and waited for him to answer.

*"Mama James, let me explain."*

*"Oh, you gon' explain alright. I'm on my way to you now, so where ya ass at?"*

*"I'm in my office at the club. Come on."*

I hung up without saying anything else to him. This man child was gonna hear what I had to say. If he wanted to work some shit out with my daughter, then he'd have to give her time. Royalty wasn't trying to hear none of what he was talking about right now. Since Royalty was staying at a hotel not too far from his club, it only took me about fifteen minutes to get there. I pulled in the parking lot right next to his car and got out. Lord forgive me for walking into this type of establishment.

"I'm sorry ma'am, but you do know this is a strip club, right?"

"I do. I also know that my son-in-law is the owner. Now if you'll excuse me," I said, side-stepping his big, burly ass.

"My bad, ma'am. It's just that you're dressed for Sunday service, and I di—"

I didn't even let his ass get the rest of his sentence out. I chopped his ass in the throat. I don't know why people keep trying to test me. Lord forgive me for putting my hands on that young man, but it served him right. These young folks out here just too damn disrespectful these days. I left him trying to breathe and walked in. I had to clutch my pearls at all the nakedness I saw.

"Mama James, come with me."

I looked up to see Duke and took hold of his arm. I

tried to focus on him, so I wouldn't see none of the naked tail that was all over the place. He led me straight to Kavion's office. I barged in and saw some stripper hoe standing in front of his desk. That didn't make things no better because all I saw was red. Before I knew what came over me, it was like I had the strength of Samson, and I snatched her up by her jacked-up lace front.

"I can't stand tramps like you. Don't you understand that man has a wife? What the hell is wrong with all you homewrecking hoes? Get ya' own man! Now take this ass whoppin' ya' mama shoulda gave ya'!" I yelled, swinging the girl around by her hair.

"Mama James! Mama James, you got it all wrong. She wasn't tryna do nothing with me. She was asking for some time off."

I heard what Kavion said and let go of the little girl whose weave I had in my hands. Well, she fell to the ground, but her wig was still in my hands. I shrugged and tossed it to the ground. I straightened myself out and turned to face Kavion.

"Considering the circumstances, you should know that anybody can catch these hands. I don't play about mine. How the hell was I supposed to know she wasn't in here trying to suck your little peter-weter? Hmmm."

"I'm not even gonna justify that with an answer. Duke, can you take Sparkle down to the locker room and make sure she straight? She can have a week off with pay."

"With payyyyyyy?!" I screeched.

"Mama James! You came to talk to me, so can we do that, please?"

"Look here, boy!" I started. "First of all, you got my daughter balling her damn eyes out because you couldn't keep it in your pants. Secondly, y'all just had a damn baby. What the hell are you gonna do to make this right before I have to put you six feet under?"

"Mama James, I love Royalty with all of me. I'll do anything to make this shit right. Tell me what I gotta do."

"First, you're gonna have to find a way to get rid of this damn club. She ain't never gonna trust you again as long as you surrounded by strippers. If you wanna keep this income coming in, I suggest you hire somebody."

"Done! I can't give up this club yet till I find a new way to make money, but I'll hire whoever I need to hire to take care of my wife and son. Where is she?"

"Somewhere your ass ain't! Y'all need a few days apart, so look here, Donell Jones, figure out where you wanna be because you ain't about to be playin' with my baby like that. Do you hear me?"

"Clearly, Mama James. Tell my baby I love her and

kiss my son for me."

"Yeah, yeah. Just do what I told you to do."

"I just have one question though."

"What, damn it?"

"Did you really have to drag that girl like that?" Kavion asked laughing.

"Damn straight I did. I didn't know what I was walking into. I'll say an 'Our Father' for that later. Let me get back to my daughter and grandson. You have one-week, Kavion. One. Week. Get it together."

With that, I walked out of his office secure in what I said and did. Nobody was going to play with Royalty Faulk and get away with it. Not on my damn watch.

# CHAPTER EIGHT

## TISHA

Savage had me and my mama fucked up! We both knew he had something to do with my Jay's death. How the fuck could my sister, have had a heart attack? Ain't no fucking way! I didn't believe that shit for one second. When I saw him and his bougie ass wife at the doctor's office, I decided to confront him. Just as I was gonna say something they got called to the back, so I rescheduled my appointment and waited for them to come outside.

As I sat in my car, I thought about all the good times I spent with my sister. Jayonna was my best friend. Shit, she was my only friend. I didn't really deal with females like that except when I had to, but my sister was cool with everybody. When she started dancing at that damn club, I knew nothing good would come from it--especially once I saw Savage. Knowing Jay, she had her sights set on him, and she was gonna get him any way that she could.

I noticed the change in her about a month ago. She started being secretive and sneaky. She was taking jobs outside the club, and I even found some powder in her purse one time that she swore wasn't drugs. Everything about her screamed she was lying, but I didn't want to make her push me away by asking too many questions. I just let her know that I was always there for her when she needed me. I knew Savage was the last one she was with because she called me that night. I didn't answer, and she left a message.

I replayed that message over and over just to hear her voice. That was part of the reason why I wanted to confront that bitch ass nigga. Her message replayed over and over in my mind.

*Sis, always remember that I love you. I just can't keep dealing with this shit with Savage. Nigga gotta whole wife at home but wanna run my life and shit. I'm meeting with him to tell him this shit is over with tonight.*

That was the main driving force behind me getting at his ass. I didn't even give a fuck if it was proven that my sister did die of natural causes, I still wanted his ass to pay for it. If it took for me and my mama to run his name and club into the ground, then we'd do that because my sister deserved justice. As soon as I saw his wife step out the door, I hopped out my car and hightailed it over there. I said what I needed to say, and that created just the type of drama I needed. My mama always told me emotional niggas always made mistakes.

I got back in my car and watched as his precious little wife screamed at him. He rubbed his hand down his face and started talking. I wish I could've been in the car to hear what he was saying. He was probably trying to make my sister out to be some thot. Not on my fucking watch. They pulled off, and I pulled out behind them. I fell three cars back and followed them to wherever the hell they were going.

This nigga was so caught up in explaining shit to his wife that he didn't even notice me. He led me right to his house. I continued to drive past him while repeating the address over and over again. I got to the end of the block and typed his address into my notes on my phone. I'd be back, and I didn't give a damn about causing any problems. One thing I knew how to do was stir up some shit. Savage was on my shit list, and he was gon' have to pay me in blood.

# CHAPTER NINE

## SAVAGE

Shit was wild. My shit finally caught up with me. This was what the fuck I got for meeting Jay's people and shit. After her sister confronted us at the doctor's office, we went home. Royalty packed up some shit for her and her baby and left. That cut me deep as fuck. I paced back and forth in my office. There was a knock, and Duke came in before I could say anything.

"Yo, it's some detectives downstairs that said they need to speak with you. It's about Aquafina."

"Fuck, man! Send 'em up. The bitch had a heart attack, so I know they ain't got shit on me."

"You sure? I know you're still pissed right now, and I don't want you to fuck around and make a mistake."

"I'm good. Send 'em up so they can hurry the fuck up and leave."

Duke walked out my office, and shortly after, he returned with two detectives. I was sitting behind my desk looking busy, but I was far from it. I got up from my chair and walked around the desk to shake their hands.

"Good evening, detectives. What can I do for you?

Would you like a soda or water to drink?"

"No thank you, Mr. Faulk. My name is Detective Ormond, and this is Detective Rafael. We're here in regards to your employee, Jayonna Morales."

"What can I help you with?"

"Around what time did she leave work that day?"

"She cashed out around her last set and then left. That was around two a.m."

"Did you know if she was going straight home or to a boyfriend's house?"

"Sir, I don't make it my business to get involved with my employees' personal lives. Unless they come to me with a situation, I don't ask, and they don't tell."

"Where were you the night Ms. Morales died?"

"I was at the hospital with my wife. She was giving birth to my son."

"Can anyone other than your wife confirm you were there with her?"

"The staff, my mother-in-law, and the doctor who delivered our baby. Is there something you want to ask me?"

"I'll just come out and say it. Was there something going on between you and Ms. Morales that would cause you to perhaps, react irrationally and do something to her?"

"Are you implying that I killed my employee? What reason would I have to kill someone?" I asked appalled.

Detective Rafael cocked her head at me. The entire time she was quiet while her partner questioned me. I didn't like the way she looked at me, but I didn't break my stare at either one of them.

"I love what you've done with yourself. You and your former boss. A reinvention, if you will. You and I both know that you can take the nigga out the street, but you can't take the street out the nigga. We have evidence that Ms. Morales had intercourse that night. We also have evidence that says you two were having an affair. Is that the reason why your wife checked into Trump Towers tonight?" Detective Rafael asked.

"Look, Detective, I had nothing to do with my employee's death nor did we have a relationship. I sent my wife to Trump Towers to relax after having our baby because I knew I'd be busy this week with my club. I didn't have to reinvent shit. I've never been arrested, not even had so much as a ticket. I consider this harassment. Please leave now. Anything further can go through my lawyer," I stated with finality.

I watched as Detective Rafael had a smug look on her face. Detective Ormond just walked off leaving her behind. He was a smart muthafucka. As soon as they were out of my office and Duke was leading them back downstairs, I called

True. I would need his brother for this one here. There was no way in hell I was about to let them pin this bullshit ass charge on me. I didn't know what stick was up Detective Rafael's ass but I didn't want to end up behind bars for nothing.

# CHAPTER TEN

## TRUE

Nigga just had to disturb my damn peace. Me, Honesty, and Faith were doing good out here in Houston. It was way different from Chicago. The air even smelled different. I had a long way to go with repairing my relationship with my daughter, but it was coming along just fine. She had a mouth on her and sometimes, I even encouraged the shit. I just wanted to enjoy my family though.

Not too long after I moved to Houston and we settled my mama's estate, Jaysa moved into my mama's house, and Jordan took over her law practice. Honesty stayed working at the law office with my brother, and I took care of Faith and Jaleel while Jaysa went back to finish medical school. I'll be damned if she didn't finish what she started all because she had a baby.

I owed it to her anyway as her big brother. I did kill the fuck nigga she got pregnant by. Jaleel was gonna be good for the rest of his life. With me, Honesty and Jordan, he was set. Mama made sure of that too. It was almost like she knew she didn't have that much time left when she found me. The small amount of time I had her, I cherished that shit. Because of her, I had a little brother and sister. My life was really good.

When Savage called me to say that Royalty had the baby, I was happy for my lil' nigga. I was all set to take my family up there in a few days so we could meet the baby and kick back. Now here this nigga goes ringing my damn line after midnight like my wife wouldn't kill me.

"Babe, who the fuck is calling you this late?" Honesty asked me.

"Chill, it's Savage."

Honesty popped up in the bed and looked at me while I answered the phone. I listened while Savage talked and just nodded. As soon as we hung up, I turned to my wife and let her know we had to go…NOW!

"Get up and get dressed. Some asshole cops are tryna pin a murder on Savage, but the news said the girl had a heart attack and crashed her car."

"So what the fuck does that have to do with him?"

"The girl worked at his club."

"Annnnddddd? Just 'cuz she worked there doesn't mean shit. What ain't you tellin' me, True?"

*Shit! I knew she'd read me like a fuckin' book.*

"He was sleeping with the girl according to what he said. The sister of the girl confronted him and Royalty when they left the doctor's office the other day. Apparently, she also went to the police and told them her sister was murdered."

"Oh, fuck no!" Honesty said, hopping out of bed.

She walked over to the dresser and grabbed some clothes out to get dressed. She slid into her sweats and threw on a pair of Uggs. She left the room to get Faith up while I called Jordan to let him know what was going on. I'd need his skills as a lawyer for this. His ass was the best criminal defense lawyer in Houston. He told me he'd be ready by the time I got to the house. He had to make sure Jaysa and Jaleel got up too.

In less than an hour, my family was ready to go. We were all in my SUV headed to my private hangar at the airport. We boarded the plane and were off. We touched down three hours later, and there was another SUV waiting for us. As soon as the stairs were let down, I stepped down them, and Savage got out the car. I walked over to my lil' nigga and dapped him up.

"What the fuck you done got into, nigga? I ain't even been gone a whole damn year."

"Man, I fucked up. I mighta lost my wife too! I just need Jordan to make all this shit go away for me. CPD got a hard-on for a nigga, especially that bitch detective that came through. She even brought you up."

"Nigga, you ain't tell me all that. I ain't tryna be in no shit up here. Honesty would fuck me up. I swear if I don't get no pussy while I'm here, I'ma fuck you up!"

"Chill, my nigga. You ain't 'bout to be caught up in no shit. This is all me."

I turned around and went back on the plane to help with the kids. Jordan grabbed Jaleel, and I picked up a sleeping Faith. We all left the plane and got in the truck. Jordan and Savage talked about what was going on as I sat in the back seat with my wife and sister. The kids were asleep in the third-row seat. I had fallen asleep myself and was shaken awake by Savage when we got to his condo.

"C'mon, nigga. Y'all can stay here while y'all in the city."

I stretched and shook Honesty and Jaysa awake. Jordan came around the back to grab Jaleel, and I got Faith. Her little skinny ass started squirming in my arms and got mad.

"Put me down. Shit! Got me woke early for no damn reason," Faith fussed.

"Lil' girl, what the fuck did I tell you about talking like that?"

"Whatever, Daddy. It's early as hell, and you wanna lecture me. Just tell me where I can go lay down at so I can go back to sleep," Faith said rolling her eyes at me.

I snatched her ass up, and she got herself together quick. She knew I didn't play that shit. I knew sometimes I thought the shit was funny and even let her do it, but it was too damn early in the morning for her to be trying me. She shut up, and we walked inside the building. Once inside the condo, Honesty took Faith, and they went back to sleep. Jaysa did the same with Jaleel giving me the evil eye. I knew she didn't wanna leave Houston, but she had no choice. Whenever I went somewhere, so did my family.

I sat in the living room with Savage and Jordan as he told us the whole story. When he was done, my mind was just blown. How the fuck do you fuck a bitch to death? I laughed so damn hard at his ass that my entire face turned red. My stomach hurt from laughing so damn hard. Even Jordan was laughing at this nigga. Savage sat there looking pissed, but I couldn't help it. He fucked a bitch into a heart attack.

"So, here's how I see things. If the cops come around you again, you give them my name and number. If they arrest you, then you call me immediately. From now on, I don't think you should go anywhere alone. You said you trust Duke so have him with you at all times. Where is Royalty at right now?" Jordan asked.

"She got a room at Trump Towers, and her mama is

there with her. That lady came to my place of business, whooped one of my dancer's ass, and then went off on me."

"Serves yo ass right, lil' nigga. I'm going back to sleep, and hopefully, I can get some pussy. Don't bother me, damn it. I'll get up when I get up."

I left Savage sitting in the living room talking to Jordan some more. This wasn't my mess, and I didn't want to be involved in it, but I couldn't leave my lil' bro hanging like that. When we woke up, I'd drop Honesty and Faith off to see Royalty and the baby and check his lil' ass out. Niggas just out here tryna live, and it's always somebody tryna fuck that up.

# CHAPTER ELEVEN

## ROYALTY

When I woke up, I almost forgot where I was. I looked around and noticed that I wasn't in my room. Memories of yesterday came flooding back to me. I got out of the bed and ran straight to the bathroom to throw up. I couldn't believe Kavion would do this to our family. I wondered how long he'd been doing shit like this behind my back. Had it been just recently? A couple years? The whole time since we'd been together? I had hella questions that needed answers, but I knew I couldn't be around Kavion right now.

I washed up and went into the living room area to find my mama and my baby. As soon as I rounded the corner, my eyes got bi,g and I took off running. I couldn't fucking believe it!!

"Sisssssss! When did you get here? Oh my gosh! We got so much to catch up on." I gushed at Honesty.

"Indeed we do. First, you can tell me why you're in this damn room and not at home?" Honesty questioned me.

"Girl, that's a long ass story."

"Well, somebody needs to tell the damn thing. I got

dragged out my bed in the middle of the night, and I'm not cut out for shit like that. You need to start talking." Faith huffed.

"Lord Jesus, help me not lay hands on this lil' girl. Who the hell am I kidding?" Mama said, snatching up Faith.

Honesty and I jumped out the way. When Honesty went to reach for my mama, I snatched her ass back. I didn't do it because I didn't want her touching my mama. I did it because she didn't want that ass whooping next. Shit, I was almost thirty, and she'd still whoop my ass, so I know she'd yolk Honesty up in a heartbeat.

"Little girl, you need to have some damn respect. You 'bout ten years old cussing like you grown. Ya' mama might let that slide, but I'll be damned if I do. Ya' mama can get some too!" Mama hollered out as she whooped Faith.

Honesty looked close to tears, and Faith's face had gone completely red from screaming and crying. She let Faith go and turned towards Honesty. I hopped out her way because I didn't want those problems.

"What the hell is wrong with you letting that child carry on like that? In order for them to do better, you gotta do better. I should whoop you because you let this happen. I don't give a dam what you can possibly say to me to make me think this is ok. Nothing you can say is acceptable at all. Sit your ass down."

Honesty sat down next to Faith who was crying. She was about to pull Faith into her lap when Mama stopped her.

"You will NOT baby that child. Now, I've already asked for forgiveness for whopping that child, but don't make me do it again. Little girl, when you're around me, you will speak like a child is supposed to. Do you understand me? I better hear yes ma'am and no ma'am from now on."

"Yes, ma'am." Faith cried out meekly.

I tried not to laugh at Honesty getting scolded. Faith was a lil' badass. If you asked me, she deserved that ass whooping. Honesty let her get away with way too much shit. True would get on her too, but not like he should either. Finally, Faith calmed down. Once I saw that she was getting along fine with my mama, I told Honesty to come down to the hotel bar with me.

"Mama, we'll be downstairs if you need us. If you want something to eat, just call room service, and if I need to come get Sir then let me know.

"Hush girl and go on. I got these babies. We just fine right here." Mama shooed me away.

I hightailed it outta there with Honesty right behind me. We wasted no time getting on the elevator and going downstairs. I needed a drink in the worst way. Once we got to the restaurant and into a booth, I spilled the beans.

"Kavion has been cheating on me with some stripper bitch from the club. She died last week, and her sister confronted us as we were leaving the doctor's office. He told me he'd been dealing with her for a few months, but she was the only one. I don't believe shit he says though."

"Get the fuck outta here! I would've never thought he'd ever do something like to you. He loves and worships the ground you walk on."

"I wouldn't have believed the shit either until it fell out his damn mouth. Where the hell is the damn waitress? Waitress!" I yelled out. I needed some alcohol.

"Good afternoon. What can I get for y'all ladies today?"

"I want a Patron margarita, and keep 'em comin'. What you gettin', Honesty?"

"I'll have the same thing she's having."

Once the waitress was gone, I continued on with my story.

"So, after the girl's sister approached us and told me what was going on, he tells me everything. He met her at the damn club, and he's been creeping around with her. He said some shit about her just being something to do. He begged me to let him fix it, but I don't know what I wanna do. We just had a damn baby for Christ's sake!"

"Honey lemme tell you something. It's ok to be

confused about loving your husband. Hell, I still loved True's ass even though one of the crazy bitches he was fucking with kidnapped me. I still loved that man ten years later, and I still love him now. You've been with Kavion since you were eighteen. Both of y'all are young, and I'm not tryna make excuses for him, but that plays a huge factor in things. Sometimes in order for y'all to grow, you have to spend some time apart."

"That's real shit, but I don't know if I want to go back to him. I just can't do it right now."

"Then don't. Don't make a permanent decision based on temporary emotions, babe. You feel the way you feel right now, and I get that, but you love that man. Take some time and figure out what you want to do. There's no rush, and don't let nobody pressure to make a decision you don't wanna make. I got ya' back, boo."

"I appreciate you so much, sis. You just don't know. I don't know how long I'll need, but I know I won't be going back to him anytime soon."

We enjoyed the rest of our drinks and had brunch while we finished talking. It was such a relief to talk to someone older than me. I loved Kaliyah to death, but she stayed in her damn phone all the time. She always wanted to record shit, but some stuff wasn't for everybody. Even

though she was making a huge wave on social media as an
IG model, I didn't want any of my life public. I had enough
shit going on as it was.

We talked a little while more and had about three
more drinks each. I was slightly tipsy and needed to sleep
this liquor off. Thank God for my mama because right now I
didn't know what I'd do. Honesty paid the bill, and we got up
to leave. Just as we walked out the restaurant, a woman
stormed over in our direction. She looked madder than a
raging bull too. She stopped dead in front of us.

"I know you know what happened to my daughter. As
God is my witness, you and your husband will go to jail for
what you've done! I'll fight to my last my breath to prove
y'all killed my baby!" she yelled at me before she slapped
me hard across the face.

All I saw was red. I was gone off the liquor too. I
snatched that woman up and beat the shit out of her. All I
remember was flashing red lights, people yelling, and
Honesty screaming my name. I didn't remember much else.

# CHAPTER TWELVE

## HONESTY

I didn't come back to Chicago for all this shit. Royalty and I were just trying to have a nice brunch and a few drinks. When we walked out the restaurant to head back to the room, some lady jumped in Royalty's face. When she slapped her, all hell broke loose! Royalty beat the shit outta that lady all through the lobby. Hotel security and a couple cops tried to pull them apart, but with the way Royalty was feeling, it took them a few minutes to do it. She was mad as fuck, and I didn't blame her for taking all her anger and frustration out on this lady whoever the hell she was.

As soon as I knew what the police were gonna do, I called True and Savage. I knew both of them weren't gonna like this shit, but oh well. If Savage woulda kept his dick in his pants, then he wouldn't have to worry about somebody coming for his wife. I pulled my phone out my purse as I watched the police place Royalty in the back of a squad car. I tried to plead with them that it was self-defense, but they weren't trying to hear me. I dialed True's number and waited for him to answer.

*"Hey baby, how's everything that way?"*

*"Babe, Royalty just got arrested. Send Jordan down to the 18th precinct to get her out."*

*"What the fuck? How the fuck did she get arrested?"*

I quickly explained to him what happened while Savage fussed and cussed in the background. This was all his damn fault anyway. I listened as he told me what to do when it came to Mama James and the baby. I decided to go upstairs and do what my husband said. I knew that all of us going down there wouldn't serve a purpose but try telling that to Mama James. She was one tough ass cookie, and I knew once she heard what happened, there was no stopping her.

I got in the elevator and went upstairs. As I trudged down the long hallway to the room, I was taken back to when I went through the shit I went through because of True. It wasn't something I relived often, but it did bother me from time to time. I knocked on the door and waited for Mama James to let me in.

"Uh, lil' girl, you left with my daughter, and now you're back without her. Where is she? Did she decide to go fuck her husband up?" Mama James laughed lightly.

"Ummm yeah, about that. When we were downstairs, some lady approached us and slapped her. She beat her up in the lobby and got arrested, so she's in jail. I already told True to send my brother-in-law down there to get her out. He's the best at what he does. True said to just sit tight and wait for his call," I told her just blurting it out.

"Like hell! I'm going where my baby is at. Lemme just get Sir ready, and I'll be on my way," Mama James said shuffling away.

I tried to do whatever I could to calm Mama James down. About three hours after I told her the news, somebody was banging on the hotel door. I went to answer it, but she pushed me back down into my chair. She ran to the door and flung it open. Royalty fell into her arms sobbing loudly. Just to see that moment made me cry. True came in behind her followed by Savage. I rolled my eyes at his ass.

"Aye, what I tell you? That ain't got shit to do with us. Just get our daughter so we can go. Don't get mad at me for what the fuck he did. You need some dick or something to make you act right? Just say the word, and I'll bend that ass over right now."

"Babe, no. I'm good. I just don't like the whole situation. It just puts me in a bad head space."

"We out," he told me before going over to Savage and saying something to him.

Savage dapped him up while I hugged Royalty. I promised to call her tomorrow, got Faith, and we left. As we rode down in the elevator, I asked my husband what he told Savage.

"I told that nigga we were coming up here to help him, but if I didn't get no pussy from my wife because of his bullshit, then I was busting his ass," True said seriously.

"Really, babe?"

"Yes, really. Fuck you thought? Just because we ain't at home don't mean I won't stretch that pussy out. I can't get enough of you."

"Ewww Daddy, I don't wanna hear that shit. If you and my mama wanna be grown then be grown but not around me, please. By the way, I like being an only child, so don't get pregnant," Faith said rolling her eyes.

"What I tell you, lil' girl? Talk to me like that again and watch me snatch ya' soul up outta you." True warned Faith.

"My bad, Daddy. I don't want them problems," Faith mumbled.

He made me blush saying what he said even though our daughter was present. He whispered some nasty shit in my ear as we waited for his car to be pulled around by valet. By the time we got in the car, my pussy was hot and ready like a Little Caesar's pizza. I couldn't wait to get back to Savage's condo to break him off. I was just like my husband, I couldn't get enough of him. We parked in the garage and damn near ran into the building with Faith trailing behind us. I was about to bust it wide open for my husband tonight.

\*\*\*

When I woke up, I smiled at the aching between my thighs. True really put it on me when we got home. I was enjoying every bit of loving he gave me. Faith was still asleep, and True was probably in the living room. I knew he had some calls to make concerning his club. He opened a club in Houston called Eve's Apple, and it was popping. I couldn't lie, True had really been doing his thing in a legit ass way since we reunited. After selling S & D to Savage, he was free to do whatever he wanted with a ton of money. My family was good for the next three generations.

I stretched and went to the bathroom to handle my business. Once I was good, I went in search for my family. I found everybody in the living room. Even though Jaysa seemed mad at first, I saw her and Kaliyah talking it up about shopping on the Magnificent Mile. They were even talking about going to Nine Mag to get tattoos. I decided to jump in on their conversation.

"When we gettin' tattoos, bihhhh?"

"We can go this afternoon. Let's just leave these niggas with the kids and go. My black card burning my pocket up right now!" Jaysa exclaimed.

"Alright, let's go, but I wanna stop at the Amazon store. I heard they got the books I was looking for by Marina

J."

"Who dat?" asked Kaliyah.

"Whatttttttt?" Jaysa and I exclaimed in unison. "She's one of the dopest authors at Miss Candice Presents in my opinion. Her, Jade Royal, Iisha Monet, and Londyn Lenz is doing the damn thing. I order all their books off Amazon as soon as they drop."

"I'ma check her and all the other ones out. If they as good as you say they are, I'ma buy all they shit," Kaliyah responded.

We all got dressed and headed out. We stopped at Nine Mag and got tattoos. I got True's name big as shit on my left titty right over my heart. If that nigga couldn't appreciate that, then I'd just have to stab his ass. Y'all think I'm playing, but I'm so serious. We did some shopping on the Magnificent Mile and went back to the condo. I didn't pay attention to what I spent, but when you're married to a boss, who does?

It wasn't until I got back home that I shot a text to Royalty to check on her. She let me know that she was alright, and I left it at that. I went to check on my baby and saw that she was sound asleep. I went back into my room and stripped so I could take a shower. Just as I was walking into the bathroom, I was roughly pulled back. A hand grabbed my throat and grasped it tightly.

"You thought you was gon' spend all day away from me, and I wasn't gon' be mad about it? Bend that ass over and take this dick," True whispered in my ear.

I did what my baby told me and assumed the position. Once I bent over the bed and arched my back, it was all he wrote. My husband dug my guts out for the next hour before cumming deep inside me. Lord, please forgive me, but that shit was so damn good.

# CHAPTER THIRTEEN
## SAVAGE

### FOUR MONTHS LATER...

I was sick as fuck without my wife! Since Tisha and her ugly ass mama decided to confront her, she'd been staying with her mama. I was missing out on time with my son and everything. I got to see him, but there was nothing like going to sleep and waking up with your family. I had sent True back home with his family once I got out that jam. The Chicago Police Department had no choice but to close Jayonna's case since she died of natural causes due to drugs.

Was her mama mad? She was mad as fuck, but there was nothing that she could do to me. She hadn't popped up or made no noise since CPD told her the case was closed. I figured shit was safe for me to move again, so I went back to work to get my mind off shit going on with me and Royalty. I was looking for a new club manager until I could sell the club. At the moment, I was looking to invest in another business to keep my money flowing. I had talked to True who told me about a restaurant that Bread and Butta's little cousin had opened in NC called Bunny's.

I wanted to open one here in Chicago, so I'd been

talking to Queen, their cousin Lazarus' wife. I didn't find out till a few months in that Lazarus had passed away. I had nothing against dealing with Queen, but I didn't need any more problems with my wife. I usually spoke to Renz who was Lazarus' grandfather. He was the one brokering the deal for the franchise for me. If all went well, I found a prime location on the west side for Bunny's.

I was trying my best to get Royalty to forgive me, but she wasn't budging. After True and his family went back to Houston, Royalty moved into the condo. I had to call before I came by, schedule time to see my son, and a bunch of other rules she had. I was tired of the shit. I decided to call Mama James and ask for her help.

*"What the hell do you want, boy? I'm trying to watch my stories, and you interruptin' me."*

*"Hey Mama James, sorry for bothering you, but I need your help?"* I asked sheepishly.

*"Help with what? Did you do what I told you to do?"*

*"I wanna take Royalty out tonight. And yes, I have interviews set up next week for a new club manager. I even been talkin' with somebody else about opening a restaurant too. I just wanna do whatever I can to ensure that my family is good."*

*"Well, good. Now, where you tryna take my baby?"*

*"There's this Brazilian steakhouse I wanna go to called Fogo de Chao. It's supposed to be good as hell, and I wanna try it out. I know Royalty likes trying new food, so I wanna take her on a date. Can you watch Sir tonight?"*

*"I'll call Royalty now and have her bring him to me. I swear if you don't make things right soon between you and my baby, I might have to cut you. I love you like a son, but Royalty came from me. I ain't got no problems with sending you to the king."*

*"Alright, Mama James,"* I said laughing.

*"I'ma try as best as I can tonight."*

I hung up with her and headed straight to Barnes & Noble. If there was one thing, I knew about my wife it was that she loved to read. Even though she was a sucker for that hood shit, she read thrillers and criminal fiction too. One of her other all-time favorite authors was James Rollins. He wrote some weird ass shit, but it was good as fuck. I literally bought every book with his name on it.

I headed straight back home to get myself together for tonight. I was lucky to get a last-minute reservation for the restaurant. I showered and got dressed. I kept it simple in a pair of off-brand ass jeans and a v-neck black tee. I stopped at Walmart and grabbed three gift bags to put all the books in and some flowers. I bought all the damn *3 Musketeers* candy bars that they had near the register. I was trying my best to win my way back into my wife's heart.

I got back in my car and headed straight to the condo. I had all three bags plus the flowers in my hands. I was nervous as shit. I didn't know if my wife would even be receptive to me right now. Hopefully he mama smoothed things over for me. I walked to the door after getting off the elevator and knocked instead of using my key. Soon after I heard the locks click and Royalty opened the door. Music came blaring out of the door, and I smelled something good cooking.

"What are you doing here?"

"I came to see my wife. I can still do that, right?"

"You shoulda called first, Kavion. I'm not in the mood to deal with you tonight. My mama took the baby, and I just want some me time."

Just as I was about to answer, some nigga walked over to the door. He was buff as shit with a damn muscle shirt on and stared me down like I was wrong for being there. I pushed my way into the condo and tossed the bags and flowers to the ground.

"Who the fuck is this?" I growled walking straight up on dude.

"I'm the nigga who's gonn—"

Before he could get his words out, Royalty pushed

her way in between us. One of her hands rested on my chest and the other on his. She looked back and forth between us, and I saw the tears well up in her eyes. The silent pleading in her face told me everything I needed to know. Was I losing my wife? Instead of being the savage ass nigga I wanted to be, I turned around and left.

Once I got back to my car, I punched the shit outta the steering wheel until my knuckles started to bleed. I deserved for my wife to be mad at me, but this? This wasn't cool at all. My first mind told me to take my Glock back up there and blow dude's fucking brains out. I knew if I did that though, I'd end up in jail and away from my wife and son forever. I couldn't afford that, so I waited.

I musta sat in my car for like three hours watching the elevator. Finally, dude walked his ass off the elevator and over to some raggedy ass Toyota Corolla. When he pulled out, I waited a few minutes then pulled out behind his ass. I would let him get a nice little head start outta here, but his ass wouldn't make it home. It was a wrap for homie. He jumped on Lake Shore Drive heading South. That was just fine by me. Once we hit South Shore Drive, he merged on to I-55. I mashed the gas and pulled up on the side of him. I rolled my window down and let my Glock sing. His car spun out and crashed into the median, but I kept going and took the first exit. I got off, hung a left, and got right back on going in the other direction. My wife was gonna hear me tonight!

***

Once I made it back to the condo, I hit one of my lil' homie's lines and told him to come scrap my shit. I left the car unlocked and the key behind the tire. I jumped in the elevator and went upstairs to where my wife was. Fuck knocking, I was using my key. I unlocked the door and barged right in. The same slow, sad ass music was playing loud as shit. When I rounded the corner, I saw my wife laying on the couch crying. I hated when she cried, so I went straight to her.

"Why did you do it, Kavion?"

"What are you talking about? I ain't did shit."

"I've been with you for over a decade. I know my husband. Please tell me you didn't kill him. That you only shot him in his leg or something."

"Fuck what you talkin' 'bout right now, Royalty! I came here to make up with you, and instead, I find another nigga with my wife. Kinda shit is that?"

"It wasn't no kinda shit. He wasn't here for what you think, Kavion. The fucking pipe burst under the kitchen sink. He came to fix it and called himself trying to talk to me, but I turned his ass down. I just wanted him to hurry up and fix the shit so he could go. He just finished when you came."

"Tell me any fucking thing! I'm 'posed to just believe that bullshit, huh? That nigga was staring me down like I interrupted some shit." I seethed.

"Bring your dumb ass on!" Royalty yelled, pushing me away from her.

She got off the couch and stomped into the kitchen. She walked around the counter and stooped down to grab something. In her hands was a navy-blue work shirt with the name Ron stitched on the front near the right-hand pocket. She tossed it at me and walked away. On the floor was a toolbox and a discarded U-shaped pipe on the floor. I checked under the sink to see that it had indeed been repaired, and my wife was telling the truth the whole time. I had let my temper get the best of me.

"I'm so sorry, bae. I swear I am," I said remorsefully.

"Bye, Kavion. I can't believe that you'd think I'd cheat on you. Unlike you, I respect the vows that I took. There's not another man that could ever make me break them. Get out."

"Please bae, I'm sorry. I'm so fuckin' sorry! I just want my wife back. Forgive me, please. I'll get on my knees till they bleed. I swear I'll never hurt you again."

I grabbed Royalty and held her in my arms as tight as I could. She sobbed heavily in my arms, and I felt bad as fuck. I just wanted to make all this shit go away. I needed my family back. Not being able to be with my wife and son every single day was killing me. I'd do whatever it took to get that back.

Royalty shrank in my arms as her sobbing got louder. I kissed her collarbone and then her neck. I trailed kisses all the way to her ear whispering that I loved her with each kiss. Slowly, her cries turned to moans. I knew that my wife needed me as much as I needed her when she tugged at my pants. It was all she needed to do. It was over with after that.

# CHAPTER FOURTEEN

## ROYALTY

While crying in my husband's arms, my cries eventually turned to moans. Even though I didn't want to, my body needed Kavion. I tugged at his pants, and he stopped to remove them. Once he stepped out of his shoes, pants, and boxers, he removed his shirt. He stood in front of me completely naked, and my pussy was soaking wet. His hands ravaged my body pulling at my clothes, and I could feel the want wafting off his body.

I quickly pulled all my clothes off so my husband could take me. Once I was completely nude, my husband wasted no time swooping me up. My legs wrapped around his waist easily. He headed down the hall for the bedroom where we barely made it before landing on the bed. He stepped back and spread my legs as he looked at my weeping pussy. His fingers slid between the folds of my slit, and I moaned loudly.

"Baby," I said breathlessly.

"Shhhhhh," he said as he sunk to his knees.

He placed his mouth on my glistening mound. I moaned loudly as soon as his tongue touched my clit. I squirmed in delight as he assaulted me orally. He gripped my thighs tightly when I tried to move. I felt a quivering in the bottom of my belly, and I knew what was coming. My orgasm erupted from my core and squirted all over Kavion's face. My hips bucked and squirmed but he held me in place as he continued.

I was completely spent. As quick as the quaking in my stomach stopped, it started right up again when Kavion slid inside of me. My breath caught in my throat as my husband sunk his dick deep in my pussy. I moaned loudly. Gripping his back, I dug my nails in as he started to hammer in and out of me.

"Kavion, shit! Don't stop, bae, please don't stop!"

"Fuck, bae! I love you, swear to God. I'm sorry. I'm so fucking sorry. I'll keep saying sorry 'til you come back home. I want you to come back home."

"Yes, a million times yes! I'll come back. Just don't stopppppp!"

I came undone all over his dick. Shortly after I came for the fourth time, Kavion erupted inside of me. I knew I was bound to get pregnant again, but I didn't care. This man was my everything. Even though people would probably think I was stupid for taking him back after his confession, I didn't care. Ten years was a long time to just say fuck it. I also had my son to think about. Kavion would be crazy to do this stupid shit again though. I'd kill his ass dead if he did.

"Bae, I got something to say. Just keep quiet and listen."

"Ok, go ahead."

"If you ever in your life cheat on me again, we're gone, and I mean that. I don't care what you say or do. No amount of time will ever make me forgive you. Fool me once, shame on me. Fool me twice, I'll never get fooled again. I'll leave your ass in a heartbeat and never look back."

"Bae, I swear I won't ever do no shit to hurt you again. I put that on everything I love."

We made love well into the night and early into the morning. If I wasn't sure about getting pregnant again, I most certainly would be after this. Life was starting to look god again for me. I had been miserable without my husband. Day in and day out just being with my son was great, but I missed Kavion terribly. This would be somewhat of a new start for us, so hopefully, he didn't fuck this up.

***

When we finally woke up, we showered together and went to get something to eat. I wanted some Golden Nugget, and there was one on Lawrence Avenue near Ravenswood Avenue. We headed there, parked and went inside. As I sat looking and smiling at my husband, I had an idea.

"Bae, we should go get tattoos. There's a few tattoo

parlors right on Broadway. Let's go after we eat."

"Tattoos? Since when did you like needles?"

"Since now. You scared?" I asked sticking my tongue out at him.

"Scared my ass! You're probably gonna be in the chair crying and shit."

Just as I was about to answer Kavion, I saw something going on in the parking lot. I saw a lady with a baseball bat in her hands, and she was getting ready to swing at a car. Upon taking a second look, it was my husband's car. Oh, hell no! I jumped out the booth like my ass was on fire and ran towards the door. Kavion had no clue what was going on, but he followed right behind me.

"What the fuck are you doing, lady?" I screamed.

"Fuck you!" she said, swinging the bat into the windshield. "Fuck your husband! Fuck everything you both stand for! Fuck it all!" she said continuing to swing.

I pulled my phone out to call 911 as Kavion tried to approach her. I explained to the operator what was going on and where we were at. Just as she let me know that units were on the way, the lady swung the bat and hit Kavion hard on the side of his head. He crumpled into a heap on the ground, and she raised the bat again. I didn't even think twice about it and ran straight at her, tackling her ass to the ground.

We wrestled and tussled around until the police showed up. I felt a pair of strong arms wrap around my waist and pull me off the lady. I saw that it was a cop and pushed away from him to go to my husband. He was still out cold and bleeding profusely from the side of his head. Paramedics were already working on him as I stood there helpless. A crowd had formed, but I didn't give a shit. All I was worried about was my husband.

"Ma'am, can you explain to me what happened? This lady claims you started a fight with her, and she was defending herself against you and your husband."

"That's a damn lie! My husband and I were inside about to order our food when I saw her outside busting our windows out on our car. I came out here and confronted her. That's when I called the police, and she hit my husband with the bat when she finished with the windows. I jumped on her after that. Ask anybody out here."

"I will, ma'am. Thank you for your statement. I just need your name and the name of your husband. You may want to call a tow truck to get your car outta here and get yourself checked out with EMS too. An officer will meet y'all at the hospital. They'll be taking your husband to Thorek."

"Thank you, sir."

The medics loaded Kavion into the ambulance, and I

climbed in behind him after informing an officer that my sister-in-law was on the way to take care of our vehicle. Once inside the ambulance, I placed that call to Kaliyah.

*"Hey sis, what's up?"*

*"I need you to go to the Golden Nugget on Lawrence by Ravenswood and get our car towed to an auto body shop. Some crazy bitch smashed all the windows out with a bat then hit your brother over the head with that damn bat. We're on the way to Thorek Hospital so meet us there when you're done."*

*"Oh my gosh! What the fuck? Ok, I'm on it. Make sure my brother is good, please. He's all I got,"* Kaliyah said shakily.

*"I got him, boo. Just handle that for me, please. I gotta call my mama."*

After hanging up with her, I called my mama and told her what happened. She was past pissed. I didn't even know who that lady was nor why she did what she did. I had a feeling she was somebody to that girl Kavion cheated on me with, but only time would tell. The fucking news said she died of a heart attack, so why the fuck was she coming for my man like this?

Arriving at the emergency room, Kavion was rushed right in and into a treatment room. I was told to stay back until a doctor had examined him. I was a hot ass mess. I was pissed, sad, upset, crying and shaking all at the same damn time. I was pacing back and forth for about an hour when I heard somebody shout my name.

"Royalty!"

I spun around to see Halo. She stalked towards me looking worried and pissed off. I fell into her arms and cried hard. She rubbed my back and led me over to the chairs so I could sit down. I was so damned nervous that I couldn't sit down before now. I explained to her what happened and she got mad all over again.

"I told that nigga that old ass lady was fucking crazy. The bitch died of a heart attack, and she can't accept that shit. It ain't nothing for me to handle a bitch, believe that! She gotta go!" Halo hissed quietly.

"Family for Kavion Faulk," a doctor announced.

We both hopped up from our seats. "That's us, Doctor."

"Your husband is a very lucky man. He does have a concussion, but luckily, the impact didn't fracture his skull at all. He's a little disoriented, and we've given him some medication to help with the pain right now. The best course of treatment for him is rest and relaxation. You can see him shortly. I'll have a nurse come to get you."

"Thank you so much, Doctor."

We sat back down just as Kaliyah came blazing through the doors of the emergency room. She ran straight into my arms as we hugged and cried. Halo stood to the side unsure of what to do. It was then that I realized that she didn't have Storm with her and neither did Kaliyah.

"Uhhh, where's Storm at?"

"Yeah, about that. She's good. A friend is watching her for me," Halo answered.

I'd save those questions for another day. I was glad that Halo was trying to get on with her life. It had been a long time since Big Storm was murdered. We all followed behind the nurse who came to get us and take us to Kavion's room. Thank God my husband was alright, but that bitch, whoever she was, had to fucking go!

# CHAPTER FIFTEEN

## LANA

"Let me the fuck outta here! I need to make a phone call damn it!" I yelled while in the holding cell.

Got damn CPD had me and life fucked up. They arrested me at the Golden Nugget after Savage and his stupid ass wife tried to attack me. I still wanted answers about my daughter, and I knew that nigga had them. There was no way I was gonna accept the fact that my daughter had a damn heart attack at the age of twenty-four. Nope! Not at all! She died from a broken heart fucking with that sorry ass nigga, and I was gonna prove it. I couldn't believe I was in jail.

"Lemme make my fucking phone call! Y'all violating my gotdamn rights! I'm entitled to a phone call!" I yelled.

"Shut the fuck up! You'll get your phone call soon. You don't get to dictate a damn thing!" Hissed a cop.

The way the cop looked at me made me shut the fuck up. I sat back down on the bench and waited to see if somebody would come for me so I could make my call. I didn't give not one fuck about hitting Savage with that damn bat upside his head. If you asked me, he deserved that shit and more. My daughter was dead because of him. Jayonna wasn't a damn crack head, coke head or pill popper before him. When the coroner told me that coke was found in her system, I knew she had to have been going through some really rough shit in order to resort to that.

Although I had my daughters young, I was still a friend to them after they got grown. They came and told me everything; including Jayonna when she started fucking with Savage. Hell, Tisha and I had met the nigga. That let me know right there that he meant something to her because Jay never brought just anybody home. She was the pickier one of my two children when it came to who she spent her time with. She told me all about Savage.

It came as no surprise to me about him being married especially since she told me he never spent the night or no shit like that. Even though he took her out, spent money on her or laced her pockets, I knew my daughter had unknowingly become the side chick. I didn't like the shit and made it known, but knowing Jay, she was gonna do what she wanted to do with her life. As long as he didn't play my baby, I was good.

When fuck ass CPD showed up at my door telling me what happened to Jayonna, I didn't want to accept it. I knew that Savage had something to do with that shit, and I'd waste my last breath telling anybody who would listen. While this nigga was carrying on with his life, I had to bury my eldest daughter. Tisha and I were still trying to deal with the day-to-day aspect of it all. I couldn't let the shit go. That's why when somebody told me him and his wife were at Golden Nugget, I didn't hesitate to go up there.

I spotted the all-black Audi A8 with the customized license plate that said, 'SAVAGE' sitting in the parking lot. This nigga was stupid as fuck to be driving around on my side of town like I didn't have an issue with him. I didn't live too far from the restaurant, so I didn't have to drive up there. I just walked the two blocks over to the restaurant and went straight to the lot. I swung first at his windshield. I was tryna make shit as hard as possible for him until he confessed to my daughter's death.

What I didn't expect was for his big ass wife to come charging at me. I think that bitch broke something when she tackled my ass after I hit Savage upside the head. Big bitch was still mad that her sorry ass husband was fucking with my daughter. Tisha told me all about how she confronted him in the parking lot of the doctor's office, and she was there. Serves her stupid ass right though. She wasn't about to live happily ever after after her husband had ruined my life.

"Morales! Time for your phone call!" an officer yelled out.

I went to the gate and had to turn around so she could cuff me before leaving out of the cell. I was led down to the front of where I was brought in at and to a phone. I spit out Tisha's number so the officer could dial it for me. I waited patiently for her to answer.

"*Who the fuck is this?*" Tisha spat.

"*Watch your damn mouth, little girl. It's ya' mama. Come get me from this damn police station. I'm at District 20 on Lincoln.*"

"*What the hell happened?*"

"*I'll tell you when you get here. Now hurry the hell up!*"

Before I could say anything else to my daughter, the fuck ass cop snatched the phone away from me. I could hear Tisha on the line still, but the cop didn't care. I glared at her ass. She was lucky I was in these damn cuffs. I didn't give a shit about hitting a cop. My life was already fucked up. I was shoved down the hallway and back into the holding cell to wait.

\*\*\*

I didn't know how long I'd been sitting in that damn cell. My back hurt, and I was still tired, but I could barely sleep. I didn't even know what time it was. I wondered where the hell Tisha was and how long it would take for her to get here and post my bail. I tried to get comfortable again, and I started dozing off.

*BAM! BAM1 BAM! BAM!*

"Morales! Wake the fuck up! Bring your ass on. You made bail."

I jumped up happy as fuck. I wasn't done with Savage or his wife by a long shot. I would find a way to get his ass for what he did to me. I collected all my personal property and signed out of jail. Tisha was waiting outside for me leaned up against her car smoking a cigarette. I walked over to her and snatched the cigarette away sucking in the nicotine and exhaling.

"Are you gonna tell me what happened, or nah?" Tisha asked.

"Yeah, but let's get far the fuck away from here first," I responded, climbing into the passenger seat.

Tisha pulled away from the police station and made a quick right so we could turn around. Once we got back on to Lincoln, we took it all the way out to Lawrence before making a left. As we rode to my house, I explained to Tisha what happened between me, Savage, and that bitch of a wife of his. By the time we pulled up to the front of my building, Tisha was seeing red.

"There's no way he's gonna keep getting away with this shit, Mama. For a nigga to have a name like Savage, why the fuck would he call the police on a woman? Shit like that irritates my soul."

Ok, so I embellished a little bit. Tisha didn't need to know that I was the one who went looking for trouble nor did she need to know that it was my own fault I was in jail. All she needed to know was that it was Savage's fault I was in there. I needed her to stay focused because whatever I planned to do next, she needed to be part of it.

"I don't know, baby, but I know we're getting close to him spilling his shit because why else would he lie on me to put me in jail? Sounds like a guilty nigga to me."

"He is guilty, and we both know that, so what are we gonna do about it?"

"I need to get him to confess that he had your sister killed. I know he did. I can feel it in my spirit. I have an idea."

I mapped out my plan with Tisha and let her know that everything she was supposed to do was vital. No matter what, she needed to always record what went on. Some kinda way that nigga was gon' admit to what the fuck he did to my child. A fucking heart attack? Nah, I just can't believe that. I was about to hit this nigga where it hurts every damn day if I had to. He was gonna feel my wrath.

# CHAPTER SIXTEEN

## SAVAGE

The noise in the room I was in was driving me crazy, but my entire body felt like it was weighed down with heavy ass bricks. I strained to open my eyes, but I couldn't. I could hear my wife crying next to me. What the fuck was going on? Why did my body feel like this? Why in the fuck couldn't I wake all the way up? I struggled to move just my hand or something so Royalty would know I was good.

"I can't believe this shit is happening Sis. I swear on my life I'll go kill the bitch myself if this has any long-term type of effect on him. Halo, what if it were worse? What would I have done then?" Royalty sobbed loudly.

"Then you woulda continued to be the wife and mother that you are while I handled what I needed to handle. That's why I'm the big sister," Halo responded.

"This shit is just so crazy. I don't even know that woman or why she did all that. The only one who can tell us that is Kavion."

"Lana," I croaked out.

"Oh, my gosh! Get the doctor, Halo!"

Royalty grabbed my hand and moved the top of the bed up so I could be in a sitting position. There was some yelling and some more shit in the hallway.

"I know you better get your bitch ass in that room and check on my damn brother! I know that!"

Seconds later, a doctor was shoved in the room with a mad ass Halo behind him. He adjusted his clothing and walked over to the bed.

"Hello, Mr. Faulk. Glad to see you awake. You suffered a concussion, and we sedated you to run a few tests. Everything seems fine, but we'll be keeping you overnight for observation. We want to make sure that everything stays ok. Any questions?"

I shook my head no, and he went to exit the room. I didn't know what the fuck Halo did to that man, but he was shook. He walked all the way on the left side of the room to get outta here. I started to laugh, but that shit hurt my damn head. Royalty put the bed back down so I could rest. Why the fuck was Lana on that bullshit? That's all I could think as I drifted back to sleep.

\*\*\*

When I woke up, my body didn't feel as heavy as it did before. My mouth was dry as shit though. I pressed the button for the bed to move up so I could get the cup of water on the stand next to my bed. Royalty stirred in the small ass chair next to the bed, and Halo was nowhere to be found. I guess Halo went home.

"You ok, bae?"

"Yeah, just thirsty."

She jumped up and got my water for me. I sipped through the straw, and the cool water instantly soothed my throat. I sipped a little more before moving the straw away from me. Royalty stared at me intensely, and I knew I had to tell her something.

"Who was that woman?" she asked with her brows scrunched together.

"That was Aquafina's mom. I don't know why her or her other daughter is coming at me this way. I swear I didn't kill that damn girl. She died from a heart attack for real. I swear to God."

"I believe you, but apparently, this woman isn't accepting that, so what do we do now?"

"We don't do shit. If she keeps harassing us like this then I'ma have to get a restraining order on her or some shit because I can't chance her hurting you or Sir. Y'all are my world."

"I know, bae, but can't you just, you know?" Royalty asked, sliding her finger across her throat.

"Calm down, killa," I said, laughing. "I don't need no more bullshit right now. If it comes down to it and I have to take it there, then I will. I'd do anything for you and our son."

With that, Royalty sat back down. I was wide the fuck awake, and my mind was running in a million damn directions. This shit with Lana and Tisha was way too fucking much. What would've happened if I wasn't with Royalty and that shit had happened? I woulda never forgave myself if she woulda got hurt. That woulda definitely made me kill Lana's ass. I contemplated a few things before reaching for my phone. I texted Halo, and instead of her funky ass texting me back, she called.

*"Welcome back, bro. I thought I was gonna have to go handle some shit."*

*"Nah, I'm good. Just a lil' bump on my head, that's all. I'll live. But aye, I need you to watch the crib for me,"* I said, hoping Halo caught on.

*"I got you, my nigga. Round the clock care?"*

*"If anything happens, let me know. I need to know everything."*

*"You know I will. By the way, I need you to come see me after you get out the hospital. I got somebody I want you and sis to meet."*

*"Word? You finally getting back out there? I'm happy for you, dawg."*

*"Shit, it's been ten years, my dude. Daddy needs love*

*too."*

    *"Daddy? Fuck outta here!"* I said laughing.

    *"Fuck off my line, bitch. Always tryna make jokes and shit. I hope your ass falls out the fucking hospital bed and breaks your ass. Simp ass nigga. Fuck you,"* Halo said laughing.

    Muhfucka really hung up on me too! I sat in the bed tryna focus on the old Martin re-run that was on the television, but after a while, my head started to hurt. Royalty called the nurse in for me, and she checked me out before giving me some medicine. I was back to sleep before she barely made it out the room. Thoughts of murder danced in my head.

# CHAPTER SEVENTEEN

## HALO

It had been a nice lil' minute since I had done anything other than raise my daughter. I mean, yeah, I got into some shit with True not that long ago, but other than that, it was all about Baby Storm. She hated when I called her that, but she learned how to deal with it. I had to tell her who Storm was to her and why she was named after her. Once I did that, she started calling me 'My Halo' every chance she got.

Baby Storm knew that I was a woman. I couldn't lie to her about that, but I did keep her conception a secret. She didn't have to know that her father was a fuck boy I got rid of a long ass time ago. That was another story for another day. I just told her that Big Storm was her mommy and that I loved her mommy very much. She took it for what it was and didn't really ask any questions. Every now and then though, she'd ask me why I didn't love anybody but her.

I loved her to death, but I knew taking care of her was gonna be a full-time job, and I didn't want to complicate shit. If shit didn't work out with me and somebody, she never knew about it. After all, that shit went down, I was really skeptical about who I kept around me. I knew True, and Honesty was thorough, so I wasn't worried about them. It took a while for me to get used to Savage being my brother and Kaliyah being my sister. The icing on the cake was finding out Kalila was my sister too, and her ass wasn't even dead!

When she walked her ass into Jayla's funeral, I wanted to kill her again myself for what she put my homie through. I watched True turn into a whole different person after she supposedly died, and it worried me a lot, but he always assured me that he was good. When he got with Honesty, I was happy my nigga was happy again. He was still an asshole but shit, he was happy, so that was all that mattered. Her and I had a heart to heart talk after she popped back up and shit been good ever since.

I started dating this chick named Anisa a few months back. When I saw her, I knew I wanted her. It wasn't until after I introduced myself to her that she let me know she could never forget me. She ran down our brief meeting all those years ago when I walked into her jewelry shop to buy a ring for Storm. I knew her ass looked familiar. Literally, her ass. I laughed at the thought that her ass was the one thing I remembered the most.

Anisa had shown me in just these few short months that I could fuck with her heavy. I just introduced her to

Baby Storm about two weeks ago. She took to her like a moth to a flame. Now I think my kid wanted to spend more time with Anisa than she did with me. I was cool with that though. To see my baby girl bond with my woman was a beautiful thing. She was watching Baby Storm while I handled this business.

I hit the block to handle what Savage asked me to handle. Pulling up on the 1400 block of North Latrobe, I found a parking spot and cut the engine. The house I was watching sat at the corner. I was dead ass in the middle of the hood. I didn't care though. Being over here reminded me of the trap I used to have right up the street on Division. Those were the times.

I sat watching the house intently. So far, all I saw was one light on in what looked like the living room. I sat there for about an hour before somebody emerged from the house and walked over to a beat-up Honda Civic. I debated on whether I should stay sitting on the block or follow the car. I said fuck it and followed the Honda to wherever it was going.

Trailing behind the car, the lady was completely oblivious that she was being followed. About thirty-five minutes later, we both pulled up in front of Savage's club. What the fuck? I decided to wait to see what she was gonna do. She got out her car and walked towards the entrance to the club. I waited to see if she went in and she did. I got out of my car and headed inside. I walked right past her and headed towards the back hallway to go upstairs to Savage's office.

As soon as I got in his office, I saw Duke sitting behind the desk with glasses on looking over some paperwork. As soon as he saw me, he removed his glasses and stood up.

"Everything good? How's Savage? I called him earlier to check on him, and he told me what the fuck happened."

"Yeah, he's good. He just got a concussion. Check it out though, Aquafina's mama and sister been causing trouble for my brother. As a matter of fact, her sister just walked her ass in here, and I don't know what she's on."

"Point her ass out," he said to me, pulling up the security cameras.

I looked slowly over all the monitors until I found her. She was sitting on a stool at the bar talking to the bartender. People told bartenders a lot of shit once they got drunk, so I had Duke call the bartender upstairs. She walked in shortly after and I gave her the play.

"You know 'ol girl who was just talkin' to you at the bar?"

"You mean the nosy bitch who keeps asking

questions about Savage?" Dyonna asked.

"Asking questions like what?"

"She asked if he was available because she wanted to talk to him about working here. When I told her that he was out for the day she asked if he'd be in tomorrow. I just told her I didn't know."

"Well, that nosy bitch is Aquafina's sister. Her mama already started some shit the last time she came here, and Savage told me he told you not to let her ass in, so she musta sent her other daughter in here. I need you to ply her ass with drinks and find out why she's really here."

"You got it, boss," Dyonna replied before walking away.

We watched the monitors closely as Dyonna slid back behind the bar and started making drinks. She sauntered over to the end of the bar where 'ol girl was sitting at and placed another drink in front of her. I had to have been there for almost two hours when my phone rang. I noticed that it was Anisa calling me.

*"Hey, baby, what's up?"*

*"What's up is I got on that lil' thing you like with those stilettos I showed you. I'm nice and ready too, baby. When will you be home?"* Anisa purred sexily.

*"Dead ass? Give me like an hour, and I'll be there."*

*"Bay-beeeeeee! Please hurry up! I don't know how much longer I'ma be able to take it before I start playing with my pussy. I'm so ready for you."*

*"Fuck baby, why you gotta do me like that? Keep that shit ready, and I'll be there soon."*

I hung up and looked back at the monitors. I saw the chick get up and stumble to the bathroom. I watched as Dyonna followed behind her. I waited, and moments later, Dyonna came into the office.

"That lil' bitch is drunk as shit. Her name is Tisha, and at first, she asked about a job. For the last forty minutes, she been goin' on and on about how her sister used to be a dancer here, and she was murdered. Those some heavy ass accusations she's throwing around, so I asked her why she thought that. She said she knew that her sister was fucking Savage, and he killed her because his wife found out. She also said she was gonna prove that shit."

"I appreciate you, Dyonna. Tell her to come back tomorrow, and she can speak to me about a job. I wanna feel this lil' bitch out."

"Bet that."

Dyonna left to go relay the message while I left some last-minute instructions with Duke. I knew he was gonna take care of my brother's club, so I wasn't worried. I left and got back into my car headed home. I was about to dive head-first into some pussy, and it was long overdue. Shit was stressful out here in these streets, and Anisa was proving to be a very much needed stress reliever. I could see something with her which is why I wanted to introduce her to the family.

# CHAPTER EIGHTEEN

## TISHA

Savage thought shit was cool. He got my mama thrown in jail and killed my sister. I refused to believe that she died from a heart attack even though that's what I was told. When the medical examiner disclosed to me that Jay had a ton of coke in her system, I knew he had something to do with it. He had my sister so doped up on that shit that she died. There was no other logical explanation to me except that he did it.

When I strolled into his club, I had a plan. I'd get a job there and try to find out as much dirt as I could on his ass. There had to be another bitch in here who could give me some tea. A nigga like Savage didn't fuck just one bitch while owning a strip club whether he had a wife or not. I was sure that I could get something, even if it was a small clue. I was determined to find out for sure what happened to my sister.

I left my house and went straight to his club. I sauntered inside and took a seat at the bar. I looked around and had to admit that the shit was nice as hell. I could see how my sister got caught up in all this shit. I turned to the bartender and ordered a long island iced tea. She slid a glass in front of me, and my drink was strong as shit. I gulped it down and signaled for another one. An hour rolled by and I was on my sixth drink. I was feeling good, and the bartender was cool as shit.

We were talkin, and she was telling me about working here at the club. I casually mentioned that I wanted to work here and asked if Savage was available for me to audition. She left to go check for me. When she came back, she told me that he wasn't available, but I could come back for an audition tomorrow. I was too geeked, so I ended up letting some shit slip out my mouth. I tried to catch myself, but I was too late. She heard me and followed me to the bathroom as I stumbled away from the bar.

"What makes you think Savage killed your sister?"

"Can I trust you?

"I wouldn't be talking to you if you couldn't. Between you and me, Savage is an asshole, and I can't stand working for him, but the money is fucking great."

"I know for a fact he killed my sister. Prior to working here she never did any type of drugs. She made her money and came home. He just didn't want his precious ass wife to find out that he was fucking my sister."

"Those are some pretty strong accusations though. Are you sure?"

"I'm positive. In fact, the reason I'm getting this job is to see what I can find out."

She just shook her head and held her hand out. I looked at her funny tryna figure out what she wanted.

"Girl, gimme your phone."

"Oh," I said, handing it to her.

She punched in her number and handed it back to me. I saw that she programmed her number under the name Juicy. When I looked back at her, she winked at me and smiled. Damn, she was gorgeous. If I was into women, she'd probably be my type.

"Make sure you call me tonight. I wanna help you because your sister was my friend."

I nodded and walked out. I knew I could barely drive, but I just needed to make it to my car. I got inside and took a deep breath. If there was a will there was a way, and I was definitely gonna find a way. I started my car up and drove out the parking lot sloppily. I think I made it about two blocks before I felt sick. I tried to pull over and open my car door at the same time, but that didn't happen at all. I ended up throwing up all over myself.

Not paying attention to what was in front of me, I kept driving. I drove my drunk ass right into the intersection and didn't see the truck until it was too late. You know they say your life flashes before your eyes right before you die, but that's a lie. All I could think of was how my mama would feel losing both of her daughters. The truck slammed into my car and skidded about fifty feet before it stopped. I heard yelling and screaming but couldn't respond back.

My car had been flipped on its roof, and I was hanging in my seat. My legs were stuck under the steering wheel, and I couldn't move if I tried. My entire body felt broken. The trucker came running over, and through blurry vision, I saw him kneel by the door of my car.

"Ma'am, ma'am, can you hear me? Help is on the way, ok? Just stay with me."

I tried to answer, but when I opened my mouth, blood spilled out of it. I felt fuzzy, and my body was numb. I mumbled, but more blood gurgled out my mouth.

*"Oh shit, I smell a lot of gas. I think the car is gonna blow up! Y'all need to hurry up and get the fire department or something out here now!"* The trucker screamed.

I heard him, but there wasn't shit I could do. I could barely breathe let alone struggle to get out the car. I heard sirens, but before they could get anywhere near me, I smelled the gas the trucker was screaming about. There was a loud whoosh, and I felt the fire before I saw it. The flames licked the top of my head and flickered down my body. I couldn't scream, and in moments, my body was engulfed in flames.

All I could think about was my mama.

# CHAPTER NINETEEN
## LANA

There was loud pounding at my door, and I was
pissed. It was almost four in the damn morning. Whoever the
fuck it was, was getting cussed the fuck out. I trudged down
the steps and flung the door open. Cuss words were right on
the tip of my tongue until I saw it was CPD.

"Fuck do y'all want now? Don't tell me that nigga
lied about some more shit and y'all here to arrest me?"

"Ma'am, my name is Detective Allen, and this is my
partner, Detective Wheaton. We're from the homicide
division. May we come in?"

I clutched at my chest and stepped back so they could
come in. Homicide? The fuck? I walked over to the living
room with the detectives following me. I sat down in the
recliner and motioned for them to sit on the couch. I looked
at them aimlessly with my hands clasped in my lap.

"Ma'am, do you have a daughter named La'Tisha
Morales?"

"Yes, I do. What is this about?" I squeaked out in a
high pitched voice.

"About two hours ago, there was an accident

involving your daughter and a man. It was near downtown right off Michigan. I'm sorry to have to tell you this, but your daughter passed away at the scene. There was an explosion before the fire department could get there."

"WHAT? No, you're lying! What kinda sick ass joke is this? Savage paid you to do this shit, didn't he? Get the fuck out my house!" I yelled.

"Ma'am, this isn't a joke, and nobody paid us to come here. Here's my card. I know this is all a shock to you, but please, contact me as soon as possible," Detective Allen said placing his card on the table.

The detectives walked out leaving me sitting there. I ran upstairs and found my phone. I dialed Tisha's number frantically. There was no way what they were saying is true. Not my baby. I just lost Jay. I couldn't lose Tisha too! I kept calling Tisha's phone, but it went straight to voicemail. I knew who was responsible for this shit. This had Savage's name written all over it. He just wanted to keep hurting me. I was gonna make him pay for this shit. Mark my damn words.

***

I must've fallen asleep while I was trying to call Tisha. When I stirred awake, it was almost noon. Dried tears streaked my face, and I was still clutching my phone. I dialed Tisha's number again but got the same thing as before. I got up, fixed myself together, and left to find my child. I scooped up the detective's card on the way out. I jumped in my car and headed towards Savage's funky ass club. I was gonna start there.

Once I got in the vicinity of the club, I saw cops still out there. I pulled over and got out so I could be nosy. The fire department was huddled near a burnt out car and were trying to pry the door open.

"Excuse me, sir," I said to the closest officer. "My name is Lana Morales. Detective Allen came to see me this morning stating that, that is my daughter's car. I want to know what happened."

"Hold on just one moment, ma'am. Let me get someone in charge. I'm just here to help contain the scene."

He jogged away and tapped an officer in a suit on the shoulder. They exchanged words then he pointed in my direction. They both headed back towards me. The officer nodded at me, and the guy in the suit stuck his hand out to me.

"Afternoon ma'am. My name is Detective Downs. Can you to step this way with me so I can discuss this with you in private?"

I stepped away from the group of nosy ass people standing near the crime scene tape. Once we were a safe distance away, the detective began to explain to me what happened.

"After patrolling the neighborhood and accessing the traffic cameras, we found that Ms. Morales drove through this intersection against the red light. It was clear that Ms. Morales was distracted in some way which probably caused her not to pay attention to what was in front of her. After interviewing several people early this morning, we were told that she was at a club down the street from here." He stopped to check his notebook.

"The club was Soddom & Gomorrah owned by a Mr. Kavion Faulk, but he was not in attendance for us to speak with him. We learned that he was hospitalized two days prior due to an attack by a woman named..." He looked down at his notebook again. "Ms. Lana Morales. That would be you, so would you like to tell me why you and your daughter were harassing Mr. Faulk, and how your other daughter ended up in this unfortunate incident this morning?"

"Are you fucking kidding me? My daughter is dead! Both of them are, and you're questioning me when you should be questioning why Kavion Faulk isn't in jail! He did this. I know he did!" I yelled at Detective Downs.

"Ma'am, your daughter was intoxicated way past the legal limit. Preliminary tests show that her blood alcohol level was 1.2%. It's very possible that in her intoxicated state, she caused this accident on her own. So far, we found nobody else to be at fault except Ms. Morales."

"That's total bullshit, and you know it! What is your badge number? I'm reporting you and every other sorry ass cop who won't listen to me when I say that this nigga killed my daughters. When I get through with y'all, won't none of y'all have any damn jobs!" I hissed.

He wrote down his full name and badge number for me and smiled when he did it. I was gonna wipe that smug ass look off his face soon. I don't know why nobody wanted to listen to me. I wasn't crazy in any kinda way. Was I grieving? Yes, of course, I was. But was I crazy? Hell no! I had lost both of my children in less than two weeks. I hadn't even finalized all the plans for Jay's funeral because I didn't want to bring myself to believe that my daughter was really gone. Now I had to do the same thing for Tisha. Savage was the reason all this happened. He needed to be in jail or dead. If I had my way, he'd be dead and soon.

I stormed back to my car trying not to break down in tears. As soon as I slid in my car, I broke down. My babies were gone! I carried them for nine months. I nurtured them, fed them, clothed them and raised them to be amazing women. I was so proud of both of them despite the fact that Jay was a stripper. We were very private people and didn't allow a lot of people into our space. That's why it shocked me when she started dealing with Savage.

He was the first person she ever brought home. Tisha didn't care for him right off the bat, but I was happy that my baby was happy. She was glowing actually. Tisha swore up and down there was something that wasn't right about him, and it caused many a argument between her and Jay. Jay wanted more with him, but he didn't, so she took it for what it was. Then she found out he was married, and it crushed her.

Tisha didn't clown her sister or kick her when she was down; she consoled her. She did what a normal sister would do. After that, Jay started becoming withdrawn and then one day, it was like she was back to her old self. Both of my girls were college students. Jay was one year away from graduating at UIC with a degree in Business Administration. Tisha was following in her big sister's footsteps at school. My daughters had bright futures ahead of them, but it was snatched away.

I drove home in a somber mood and made the calls I needed to make to go forward with Jay's funeral and start on Tisha's. Once I buried my children, I would stop at nothing to make sure Savage took his last breath. On God, I was gonna kill that man.

# CHAPTER TWENTY
## JAYONNA

*I never expected to die from doing a little coke. It was the only way I could cope with Savage and his bullshit. When I started working at his club, I never imagined that I would end up being a side bitch. Hell, I didn't even know that he was married. All I knew was that I was trying to save up money for my store that I wanted which led me to auditioning at his club. When I saw him, my panties got wet immediately. I pulled out all my tricks when I was dancing, and next thing I knew, I was the new headliner.*

*The dancing part came easy; concealing my relationship with Savage didn't. I wanted to flaunt it to the hating ass bitches at my job. Every last one of them had talked about throwing the pussy at Savage at one time or another. A few of them even speculated that he had to be gay if he owned a strip club and didn't even sample the pussy in it. I wanted to shout at the top of my lungs that he was all mine, and he didn't fuck with basic ass bitches, but I chose to be classy.*

*Imagine my surprise when one night he had the club shut down for the anniversary of the club, and it was an invite only party. All of us dancers were excited because he had never done anything like it before. We knew everybody who was anybody that had money would be there, and we'd get paid. He even had mock paparazzi outside with a red carpet and everything. Once everyone was inside, Savage got on stage and gave a speech.*

*All the dancers were sitting at the tables in front of the stage designated for us. He hired strippers from the most prominent clubs in the country to come out as the entertainment for the night. He wanted all his employees to enjoy themselves. He stepped up on the stage looking really zaddyish in all-white. He grabbed the mic and started.*

*"I wanna say thanks to everybody for this year of success. When a nigga like me who don't know shit about running a business can make some shit successful, it's another win for a black king like me. And what's a king without his queen, right? This year has been crazy, and at one point or another, I thought I would lose it but my baby been holding*

*I almost jumped out my chair because I knew he was talking about me, but then the spotlight came on, and it was shining on some bitch sitting in VIP. She was cheesing extra fucking hard at my man. I turned to him giving him the evil eye, but he was caught up in her. I was past pissed.*

*"Clap for my beautiful ass wife, y'all! Don't she look*

*good? Come up here, bae.*"

*She sashayed her fat ass down the steps at the VIP area and walked proudly to the stage and up the steps. As soon as she was at his side, he wrapped his arms around her waist and kissed her so deep it made me wanna snatch her ass away from him.*"

*"When I tell y'all this woman has been my saving grace from the day I met her and I wanna celebrate our good news with everyone. I'ma be a daddy, y'all! So everybody, eat up, pour up, and turn up. It's a party!"*

*They stepped off the stage, and people swarmed them congratulating them. I didn't want to seem fake as fuck or show my hand, so I did what everybody else did. I wanted to claw his eyes out at the fact that he was happy as fuck with this fat bitch flaunting her around and shit. I guess I couldn't call her fat since she was pregnant but fuck that because she still didn't have shit on me. I headed straight to the bar and decided to get faded.*

*That night, I ended up hooking up with some random and fucking his brains out after popping an ecstasy pill and snorting a line. The sex was fucking amazing! That night became the night I got addicted to coke. It started with a line here or there before I had to deal with Savage. After that whole thing at the party and me confronting him about having a wife, I tried to hide my feelings and tell myself it was just a sex thing.*

*As hard as I tried, every time I linked up with Savage, my feelings came out. He didn't make shit any better because he showered me with time, affection, and money. When we were together, he made me seem like I was the only woman in his life, so I held on to that shit like my life depended on it. I stopped giving a fuck about his wife and didn't care that she was pregnant. I fucked him like I had a point to prove every single time.*

*When his wife was about eight months pregnant, I remember her coming to the club. She was there only briefly before she left again, and right after that, I was called to his office. I fucked him on his desk with the door wide open not giving a fuck who might see. That was the first night he kissed me. To me, kissing was intimate, and you didn't do that with everybody. He fucked me aggressively as his lips pressed against mine. I bit his bottom lip, and he moaned loudly.*

*He pulled his dick from me and turned me around. He slapped me on my ass, and I made it clap for him. He told me to go close and lock the door, so I did. When I turned around, he was standing ass naked with his dick standing at attention.*

*"Come suck this dick."*

*I did exactly what he wanted and made his dick*

*disappear down my throat. I felt him grab my hair and start fucking my face. Slob ran down the sides of my mouth as I sucked his dick real sloppy. He loved that shit. He pulled me up by my hair and made me stand up. He pushed me over to his desk and leaned me across it. This was my favorite position, and he knew it. He slid into me from behind, and I came instantly.*

*His dick slammed into my pussy over and over again creating nothing but pleasure. I threw my ass back at him, and he went harder. One of his hands gripped my waist while the other one gripped the back of my neck. I was in heaven, and I felt my orgasm building up again. I came, shuddering heavily, and right after, so did he. He pulled his dick from me, and that's when we realized he hadn't put on a condom.*

*"Fuck, shorty. You gon' have to get a Plan B pill. I forgot to put on a rubber."*

*"Why though? It ain't like you can't afford another baby?" I said pissed off.*

*He grabbed me by my throat, and that was the first time he ever did some shit like that. I was beyond scared of his ass right then.*

*"Just because I can afford some shit doesn't mean I wanna have a damn football team running around this bitch. Besides, the only one having my seeds is my wife. You ain't*

*her, so don't even say shit about her, shorty. Just do what the fuck I said."*

*The next day, I did what he told me to do, but I stayed away from his ass. The night I died was the first time we talked in any way in over two weeks. I had snorted several lines before coming to the club, so I was feeling right. When I got to the club, I popped a pill and did a few shots. My body was feeling lovely, and I was up first to do my set. I had gotten ready in my outfit, and the DJ cued me up. I stepped out on the stage looking like a beautiful ass Black Barbie. I strutted down the stage looking for a thirsty ass nigga because I was about to really put on a show.*

*I stepped to the edge of the stage and rolled my hips seductively and swinging my hair around. I dropped down on all fours and popped my ass making a guy in front of me stand up and start making it rain on me. Whistles and claps were loud as I went into a split on a handstand. I popped my pussy right in his face, and he leaned in smiling. I grabbed his head and grinded my pussy on his face. The club went crazy, and that's when Duke came and snatched him away from me.*

*Pissed, I stormed off the stage and up to Savage's office. I didn't give a fuck what it looked like because I was about to show my entire ass! I busted into his office and went off. He shut my ass right up and pushed me on to the desk with my back facing his. He slid my skirt up and roughly entered me. I was pissed but angry sex was the best. I didn't protest it because I wanted it.*

*As Savage stroked me, I felt my chest tighten up. I tried to say something, but it was like I couldn't catch my breath. I pushed back at him, but I guess he thought I was trying to throw my ass at him, so he grabbed the back of my neck and went in on me. My chest felt like it was about to explode. I couldn't say or do shit. Slowly, my life slipped away from me. Tears fell from my eyes as Savage finished then pulled himself from me and walked away.*

*I took my final breath laying face down on the desk of my lover. All I could think about was how fucked my life had become because of this man, and what was even more fucked up was, I still loved him.*

# CHAPTER TWENTY-ONE
## ROYALTY

Kavion was finally getting out the hospital. I was ready to go home any damn way, and I was missing my son. Sir was with my mama, and she fussed at me because I kept calling her nonstop. New mother shit. She even blocked my ass because she said I was calling too much. I stopped calling her when Kavion started laughing at me. Big head ass nigga.

"Shut up laughing at me like you ain't in here looking like Martin after he tried to fight Tommy Hitman Hearns. Got your head lookin' all swole and shit. You better be lucky. I love your ass." I clowned him.

"And you love my swole head ass. Now shut up and help me get dressed. You know I'm handicap."

"But does that dick work though?" I asked seductively.

Kavion gave me a look that told me he'd fuck me right where he stood. My pussy got wet instantly. I started to say fuck it and bend over the bed rail for his ass, but I was stopped by the nurse who decided to come into the room.

"Good morning Mr. Faulk. I'm Nurse Ashlynn. The doctor said it was ok to release you so I just need you to sign a couple forms and you can go." She said cheerily.

I noticed the bitch lean in a little too close to my husband, so I cleared my throat.

"Excuse me, Ashy, is it? Back your funny looking ass the fuck up before you end up the next patient in this room, mmkay?"

"Ma'am, I would never!" Ashlynn exclaimed.

"And I would never let a gutter rat ass bitch even try it. You walked in here switching harder than a bitch on RuPaul's Drag Race with that sorry ass lace front on thinking you could smile in a married man's face, and it would be all good. You ever heard of Passion Provoked Manslaughter? Try that shit, and it's gon' happen tuh-day!" I spat.

Kavion was suppressing his laughter, but I was dead ass serious. I was so serious when I told his ass I'd kill him if he ever cheated on me again. Him and the next bitch would have to do what Erykah Badu said and meet next lifetime fucking with me. Kavion was mine. Forever.

He scribbled his name on the discharge papers while I eyeballed the shit outta the nurse. Wasn't no slipping him shit discreetly fucking with me. I snatched the papers out of her hand and tossed her pen at her. I grabbed hold of the wheelchair that had been wheeled in the room and pushed his ass down in it. Just that fast he had pissed me off again. I left the room wheeling him to the elevators and mashed the button.

"Bae, you good?"

"Shut yo' ass up, Kavion 'fore you don't make it home."

He shut the fuck up as we got on the elevator. I pressed the button for the ground floor and waited patiently like I hadn't just threatened his life. When I wheeled his ass out the elevator I made sure to bump into everything in our way to the door. He grunted but didn't say shit. I left him sitting by the entrance while I went to get the car. When I came back, Nurse Ashy was in his face just a cheesin' and grinning like I didn't already tell that hoe what it was.

"Come with me. Hail Mary. Nigga run, quick, see. What do we have here now? Do you wanna ride or die? Riiiiiiiiide!" I sang walking up to Kavion. "And what the fuck do we have here? You got a death wish, hoe?" I said turning to the nurse.

"No, ma'am. I'm just doing m-my j-job. I had to make sure he got downstairs safely. It's protocol." Nurse Ashy stammered out.

"Fuck your protocol and you. I told you I got this, but you just had to come on down here. Does this look like the Price is Right to you?" I said reaching into my Birkin bag.

This bitch literally had about two seconds to get gone before I aired her ass out. One thing I learned about fucking with Kavion was that bullshit walked and money talked. I could throw all kinds of cash for an incident to disappear. I snatched Kavion out the wheelchair and pushed him towards the car.

"Get the fuck in before yo' lil' girlfriend gets her edges pushed back permanently, my nigga!" I yelled at him.

Kavion laughed and got in the car like shit was all good. I hopped in leaving the nurse looking shook. I pulled off not giving a fuck about the speed limit and turned out the lot. I looked at Kavion with the side eye, but all he did was laugh.

"Real talk, you got my dick hard as fuck right now, bae. I love it when you get territorial. I can't wait to get you back home. I'ma give you all this dick and then some."

"Fuck you and your dick, Kavion. You on punishment."

"I'ma grown ass man. Fuck I look like on punishment from my own damn wife?"

"Like a nigga that got a lot of making up to do, so shut the fuck up."

So he shut the fuck up, and we rode home. I tried calling my mama so I could pick Sir up, but she still had my ass blocked. Kavion called her, and they were just having the jolliest conversation before he hung up and told me she was keeping Sir another night. Fine, whatever. I needed some sleep any damn way. When we pulled up in front of my building to go to the condo, Kavion looked at me funny.

"Fuck we doin' here? I thought we were going home?"

"My mama got the baby, you just got out the hospital, and your crippled ass can't drive, and I'm muhfuckin' tied, nigga. Shut up and get the hell out the damn car and let's go."

"I can drive this dick into you though."

"Nah, my nigga. I meant what I said. You on punishment."

"The fuck? Fuck what you talkin' 'bout, Royalty? You better gimme that shit. Stop fucking playing with me. A nigga coulda died, and you gon' deny me my right as your husband? I can't make love to my wife?"

"Here you go with yo' extra dramatic ass. I swear you be doin' the most. Come the hell on, Keith."

"Hold the fuck up! Did you just call me Keith?"

"Yep, sure did 'cuz yo ass soundin' like his whiny ass right now."

"Lord, I pray for my wife right now because she'll be there to see you shortly. She out here callin' me another nigga's name like she don't know I'm crazy. Forgive me for my sins because when I find Keith, I'ma kill his ass too.

Amen."

"What in the hell are you doing, Kavion?"

"Praying for you and Keith before I kill both y'all asses. Two days, woman! I was only in the hospital for two days, and you already got another nigga? I thought after we made up we were good, but you calling me Keith like it's ok."

"Keith Sweat, dummy. He's the only whiny ass nigga I know besides you. Stop being stupid all your life and learn some shit. Bring your ass on if you want some pussy. You eatin' ass too! Know that!"

Kavion stood there looking like a big, damn dummy while I kept walking mumbling about some damn Keith. I play Keith Sweat all the damn time in the house. You would think his ass woulda caught on, but no. For somebody so smart, he was so stupid sometimes. He finally followed behind me and stood at the elevator looking lost. He didn't say anything to me, and I didn't speak to him either. The elevator dinged, and we stepped inside once the doors opened. As soon as the doors closed, he was all over my ass.

"You think that shit funny, Royalty?" he asked, pushing me against the wall. "I'm 'bout to fuck yo' whole life up with this dick. You gon' learn today."

He grabbed my neck and kissed me deeply. I moaned

loudly, and my pussy started leaking. He kissed me like he'd just come home from doing a ten-year bid. I wrapped my arms around his neck and deepened the kiss. I felt his hard dick poking me in my stomach and couldn't wait to get inside our place. The elevator dinged letting us know we reached our floor. We were still wrapped up in each other when somebody said something.

"Oh, my dear God, Suzie, don't look at this atrocious display of vulgarity. This is just preposterous!"

"Shut yo' ass up, Becky. Let Suzie look all she wants to. She likes black dick anyway. Yo' daughter be skippin' school and lettin' Lil' D run all up in her ass. You ain't notice how her hips are spreading? You better learn about your child. Besides, she eighteen, so she was gon' start fuckin' soon anyway. But lemme tell you something, Suzie. This one here is mine, so fix ya' damn eyes before I make you legally blind," I spat at my prissy white neighbor.

Suzie giggled as her mom turned red in the face. I turned around to walk away, and Kavion was standing there biting his lip and looking at me. He smacked my ass as I walked past him and followed behind me. As soon as I got the door open, we were all over each other. Clothes flew off, and we barely made it to the room. Kavion licked me from the bottom of my feet to my neck. I pushed him forward and made him stop.

"Let's go to the room, bae. I wanna do you right."

He smacked my ass again and did as I asked. He wrapped his arms around my waist as we walked up the stairs. He placed kisses on the back of my neck as he held me in place. We made it into the room where he laid me down gently and spread my legs. Starting at the heel of my foot, Kavion kissed me all the way up my legs. He played with my pussy while he teased me and made me squirm. I exhaled and squealed in delight as he took me to higher heights.

He finally dove into my pussy, French kissing it like he had a point to prove. He slid a finger deep inside my pussy curving it to hit my g-spot, and I damn near flew off the bed from the orgasm I had. The heat in my belly spread throughout my core and spread down my legs. I was in bliss. Tears stung my eyes as the waves of ecstasy rolled over my body. Kavion stood up and wiped my pussy juices off his face. He climbed on the bed, and in one swoop, he was inside me.

The feeling was something I could never get used to, but I loved it at the same time. Every time with Kavion felt like my first time. After all, he was my first everything. The way he made my body feel each time we had sex was out of this world. This was life right now, and I'd be damned if I lost this.

# CHAPTER TWENTY-TWO
## SAVAGE

After giving my wife that knockout wood, I watched her sleep. I knew I was foul as fuck for fucking with Jayonna. That was on me. The one thing all this shit taught me was that nothing was worth my family. If Royalty had stuck to her word and really left a nigga, I'd be lost as fuck. My wife and son meant everything to me. There was no way I'd ever jeopardize that again. My days of cheating were over.

I rolled a blunt while I thought about how shit was going when my phone rang. Royalty stirred but didn't wake up. It wasn't shit but Halo anyway.

*"What's good, my nigga?"*

*"Bruh, you ain't gon' believe this shit?"*

*"What happened?"*

*"That lil' bitch Tisha came to your club last night. She was asking questions about you and throwing around accusations. I got Dyonna on her to make her talk and shit but, we don't need to worry about her ass ever again."*

*"Oh, word? Why is that?"*

*"The lil' bitch got so fucking drunk last night that her ass ran a light and got smashed up by an eighteen-wheeler around two or three this morning,"* Halo told me in

excitement.

*"Get the fuck outta here, man! How in the fuck? I swear I got an angel looking out for me or something. Look at God."* I cracked a joke.

*"Nah, that wasn't God. That was her drunk ass. That's what she get for trying you. I bet that hoe put some respeck on your name now."*

*"Yousa a fuckin' fool, man, but I appreciate that info. Now all I gotta worry about is their goofy ass mama minding her own damn business, and I'll be all good. Her ass better pray that she leaves me alone because I ain't wrapped too tight right now."*

*"You good. Now let me go 'cuz I got some ass to tap,"* Halo responded.

*"You ain't even...you know what? Never mind. I ain't even 'bout to start with yo' ass right now."* I chuckled.

*"Bye, bitch. Always tryna say some slick shit. I hope yo' dick stop working since you worried 'bout mine."*

Halo hung up on my ass, and I laughed. Soon, I was laughing so loud and so hard that Royalty woke up. She cocked her head at me looking at me crazy 'cuz I was just laughing and didn't say a word.

"The fuck wrong with you? Did that hit to the head do more damage than we thought? Lord, please don't let my husband be retarded. I mean, I already know he ain't got 'em all, but I don't need to be raising his overgrown ass."

"Look here, woman, I ain't retarded. I was just laughing at my luck."

"Your luck?" Royalty asked.

I ran down everything that Halo told me. When I got finished, the look on my wife's face said it all. She was happy and pissed at the same time. I knew she wanted to beat the shit outta Tisha because her ass had violated more than once. Now fate had intervened and did the job for her. It was what it was though. Now that Tisha was no longer in the picture, we could get on with our lives.

"Hurry the fuck up and smoke, my nigga. I want some more dick. You know when you smoke, yo' ass be ready to dick me down all night. She ready," Royalty said, clapping her hands.

"Bet that shit. Lemme smoke this, and I got you. Bring that ass over here, girl."

"I love you, Kavion. I love you from the depths of my soul. When you told me that you cheated on me, I was ready to take you to the king. Dead ass. But I loved you more than I wanted to focus on your fuck up. Now that all of this is behind us, I want us to move on. No more bullshit, just us. You cheat again, and I'll be planning your funeral."

I gulped hard because I knew she wasn't playing.

Being with me all these years had taught Royalty a thing or two. I didn't put a thing past her because I knew she was thorough. Ten years was a long ass time to learn and grow with somebody, and Royalty had definitely learned some shit. I was just glad that she was mine, and shit was gonna stay that way. She was the only one woman I'd ever loved this way. Besides my sisters, no one had me like she had me. A nigga was grateful.

I smoked my blunt while Royalty laid on my chest. All that shit talking, and her ass done fell back to sleep. I was 'bout to wake that ass back up though. I slid from under her and went to take a piss. I walked into the bathroom and drained the main vein. When I walked back in the room, I saw that Royalty had rolled over, and her ass was in the air. My favorite. I walked over to the bed, positioned myself, and slid right in. I moaned loudly. My wife had the best pussy ever. Her ass woke right up.

"Damn bae, that pussy grippin' like a muhfucka. Arch that shit," I said, tapping her on the ass.

Doing as she was told, Royalty put an arch so deep in her back that a nigga was seeing stars and shit. I stroked my wife slow and deep. Her pussy was gripping the shit outta my dick, and I had to will myself not to bust quick. I kept my concentration and stroked the fuck outta her. It had been a good minute since Sir hadn't been in the crib, so I was gon' take advantage of the shit.

"Fuck bae, you love this dick?" I whispered in her ear.

"I love that dick, bae. Shit nigga, right there!" Royalty screamed out.

"What you 'bout to do?"

"I'm 'bout to cum all over that big dick."

"Who's dick is this?"

"That's my dick, bae. All my dick."

"Who pussy is that?" I asked her.

"Yours, baby. All yours."

"That shit belong to me?" I asked, smacking her on the ass.

"Yasssss!" she screamed out.

She creamed all over my dick as she screamed out loud. I knew that when I busted this nut, my wife was gon' get pregnant. I was good with that though. I wanted another baby any damn way. I long-stroked the fuck outta Royalty until she came again. Once she came, I let myself go and shot the club up. Yeah, she was definitely gonna be pregnant again.

# CHAPTER TWENTY-THREE
## LANA

Planning funerals for both of my daughters had me fucked up in the head. First, it was Jay and now, Tisha. My entire fucking reason for being was gone. I knew I wasn't one of the best moms in the world, but to my two daughters, I was the best I could be for them. They were always taken care of even if I didn't take care of myself. I was proud of the women they were becoming because they had broken a cycle.

I didn't want either of them to be a teen mom like I was. That shit was hard as fuck. It was already hard to be black but being black and a teen mom was something else. I was determined for my daughters not to become statistics. Both of them were in college and doing big shit. Now all that was gone because of a fuck nigga named Savage. Nobody could convince me otherwise.

I made the call to the funeral home to let them know I wanted to move forward with the funeral. I also had to tell them to get Tisha's body as well. I let the director know that I wanted a double funeral so I could bury my babies together. Calling my family was the next thing to do. I only fucked with my sister and like three cousins. I called them to let them know what happened and that was that. I set the funeral for Saturday which was five days away.

Now that business was handled, it was time for me to figure out how to handle this bitch ass nigga. He took both my girls from me and for that, he had to pay. If it wasn't for him fucking with Jay's head the way he did, she wouldn't be dead now. Then Tisha just wanted to get retribution for her sister, and he killed her too. Fuck what the doctors or police would say about me right now. I'm a grieving mother. My entire family is gone. They weren't coming back and somebody needed to go to jail because of it.

The more I thought about the shit, the more upset I became. How the hell was this nigga not in jail right now? I picked up the phone and called an old friend of mine. Once she answered the phone, we talked for a lil' bit before I really got to what I wanted.

*"So, check this out. I got a problem with this lil' nigga that one of my daughter's was fucking with. I think he killed my daughter, and I need your help."*

*"First of all, how do you know he killed her? Secondly, who is this bastard?"* she asked.

*"The doctor tried to tell me Jay died of a heart attack, but my baby was only twenty-four. Then he told me she had cocaine in her system. That has his name written all over it. I know he was in the streets before he bought that damn club.*

*Shae, I swear, I want this muthafucka gone."* I spat into the phone.

*"I heard all that shit you talkin', but you still ain't tell me his name, damn it. I can't help you if I don't know who the fuck I'm looking for."*

*"His name is Savage. He owns Sodom and Gommorah strip club downtown. Tisha was out there the other night tryna find some shit out. She died in a car accident this morning. Jay died in a car accident almost two weeks ago. I think the shit is connected."*

*"Tell me what you need me to do."*

*"I just need you to help me find some information I could use to put that nigga in jail."*

*"I'm on my way, bitch. Have my drink ready."*

I hung up the phone satisfied. I knew that once Shae got here, we'd get some shit together. One thing I knew about Shae was that she knew some of everybody in the city. When you on that shit, you get to know who's who and what's what. We grew up in the same neighborhood. After YG stopped fucking with her was when she got on that shit. I did the opposite. I let my daughters be my motivation to do better.

I did a few things I wasn't proud of back in the day, but my priority were my kids. After their bum ass daddy left me for another bitch, I did what I had to do. Thankfully, I never turned to drugs, but I did turn a trick or three. Don't fucking judge me. You don't know my struggle got damn it. Anyway, my daughters were well taken care of and didn't want for shit.

Shae got there an hour later. We caught up for a lil' bit. She told me that her kids stopped fucking with her a long ass time ago when she got on that shit. Last she heard, her son had taken her youngest daughter and came up. She sounded like one cold-hearted ass bitch because she honestly didn't give a fuck about her kids. Oh, the fuck well. It wasn't my issue to worry about. I decided to get down to business.

"So, what I need you to do is to reach out to your contacts and find out what you can about this nigga. I want him gone and the sooner, the better."

"I can do that, but lemme ask you something. What's in it for me?"

"Here the fuck you go. What you want, Shae? I ain't got a lot, but I can break you off with a piece of change for your troubles."

"How much you talkin'?"

"You good with ten thousand, or you need more?"

It was like her eyes lit the fuck up. Maybe she was tryna figure out how much crack she could get with that amount of money. I didn't give a fuck as long as she agreed to do the shit.

"Ten thousand? You really got that kind of money? I'ma need a down payment."

"I ain't got the check yet, but I had life insurance on both the girls. The check for Jay was cleared already, and the company called me to say it's been sent. When I get that, I got you. Can you hold off till then, or you gon' start right away?"

"You need information, right? Lemme do what I do and just have my money when I come back. Gimme another drink before I leave."

This lil' demanding bitch! I swear if I didn't need her ass, then she wouldn't be here. I had tunnel vision right now, and all I saw was Savage's head on a platter. Come hell or high water, I'd have his ass by the balls soon. I made Shae another drink and brought it to her. I gave her about a hundred dollars just for coming through, and she ran out my house like her ass was on fire. Bet she was on the way to get her a fix right now. I didn't care either way as long as she did what I needed her to do.

I made myself a drink and sat back down. I pulled a pack of Newports out my purse and opened them. It had been a long ass time since I smoked a cigarette. I almost felt pushed to try some shit stronger than nicotine, but I didn't. I needed to be focused on making Savage pay for what he did, not chasing my next high. For right now, this Newport would do the trick.

I zoned out, and before I knew it, I had drank a whole bottle of Patron and smoked damn near the whole pack of cigarettes. I was in my feelings heavy. It was like the realization hit that both my babies were really gone. For twenty-four years, I had been a mom. My kids were supposed to bury me, not the other way around. I pulled out my phone and went to my picture gallery. I scrolled through all my pictures of me and the girls. We could pass for sisters because I was so young, but I never acted like a big sister to my kids. I was their mom, and I loved the hell outta them.

I would never get to see them get married or have babies. Hell, I wouldn't even get to see them graduate from college. Oh God, this shit couldn't be real. I was having a mental breakdown, and the most fucked up part about it was I didn't have anybody I could call to comfort me. I didn't have a man because I was at a stage in my life that I just didn't wanna fuck nobody. I didn't have to be a man's wife, but I wanted to have something stable.

I cried for what seemed like forever reminiscing on all the good times we had. I stumbled drunkenly to my room and fell across my bed. The last thought I had before I passed out was Savage sitting in a jail cell. With that, I fell asleep with a smile on my face. His time was coming soon enough. I'd make sure of it.

# CHAPTER TWENTY-FOUR
## MS. FAULK

I never got a chance to make some shit right with my son. I knew I fucked up as a mom, but I was in my feelings, and I let a lot of shit get the best of me. Instead of focusing on my children like I should have, I turned to drugs after Savion left me. That man, oh that man! You ever been loved on so good that you knew it didn't matter what happened you'd love him forever? That's what it was like for me with Savion.

I was so stuck on Savion when we met. He was someone all the girls in the neighborhood wanted, but he chose me. Back then I was a good girl. I went to school and minded my business. Most girls my age were outside all the time showing their bodies off but not me. I was really shy and low key. I went to school and came home. I never roamed the streets or got into any trouble.

I met Savion one time when I went to this lil' barbecue restaurant on Rogers. It was a new spot, and I heard the food was good there. I walked the few blocks from my apartment building and went there. Once I ordered my food, I sat down and waited for them to call my number. To pass the time I brought a book with me to read. The Coldest Winter ever seemed to be what a lot of people were talking about, so I checked it out from the library. It was pretty good so far.

I was just minding my business when I felt somebody standing over me. I looked up, and there he was. He made my body feel things I never felt before all just by looking at me. I was stuck and didn't know what to do. He smiled at me and took a seat across from me. We talked a lil' bit before my number was called. He got up and got my food for me. He brought it back to me, and we continued to talk. He was pretty smooth and had me blushing like a Cheshire cat.

Some girls came in there tryna talk to him, but he snapped telling them to take their asses on. They did as they were told, but they stared me down. I stared back at their asses because I wasn't scared worth a damn. Just because I was quiet didn't mean I didn't know how to fight. When you grow up with nothing but boy cousins, you learn a thing or two. I had heart, and he saw that shit. After that, we were inseparable. Where you saw him, you saw me.

When I got pregnant with Kalila, he was ecstatic. He showered me with money and gifts. He made me feel like the most beautiful woman in the world even though I felt like a whale. Savion was always doing shit for me to make me feel good and I was so in love with him. Right before Kalila was born, he moved me into my own place. He said it was for us, and I was genuinely happy.

Raising Kalila with the man that I loved was a beautiful thing. I had everything I wanted, and I wasn't even eighteen yet. At eighteen, when I got pregnant with Savage was when shit hit the fan. I'd never forget Kalila's birthday party when Savion's wife showed up with a kid. I was past pissed off, and there was nothing he could say to me in that moment. I think what had really pissed me off was the fact that the shit happened at my baby's party.

I was pregnant and mad as hell. Savion wouldn't let me fight, and I had to pretend that shit was ok for my baby's sake. I hid my feelings for the rest of the party, but as soon as we got back home, I let loose. I screamed, cried, shouted, and some more shit. How could he do this to me? I never knew a love like Savion before, and now I was sure I never would again. When I gave birth to Savage, he showed up at the hospital with his ugly ass wife.

All hell broke loose in my hospital room, and I had to get security to remove her. Our shit was never the same after that. Savion kept taking care of us, but I was still pissed at him. I was at a point in my life that I had two children to take care of, and I knew I couldn't do that on my own. I sucked my feelings up and allowed Savion to be part of our lives.

The visits started coming less and less, but my bills were always paid, and the kids needs were always met. We still had sex from time to time, so it didn't surprise me when I found out I was pregnant with Kaliyah. It wasn't like he was trying to use protection, so pregnancy was inevitable. I told him about being pregnant with Kaliyah, and it was world war three. He flipped out on me telling me he was trying to fix shit with his wife. I could give a fuck less about his wife and what they were trying to do. The way I looked at things, it wasn't my fault they were having problems, it was his.

Apparently, all the outside babies Savion had caused his wife to commit suicide. He was grieving and came to my house after her funeral. I tried to console him, but I really didn't want to. Why the fuck would I console him about a bitch I didn't care for? After that happened, it seemed like our relationship was back to the way it was before all the drama. He was spoiling me again and doing all the shit he used to do. Then one day, everything just stopped, and he disappeared on me. The money never stopped though.

Every month, like clockwork, there was an envelope full of money shoved under my door. It was more than enough money to pay the bills and take care of the kids. At first, I would make sure my kids were straight before doing anything else with the extra money. I started out smoking weed, and for a while, that took away the bullshit. When weed stopped doing the job, I moved onto something stronger. Cocaine did the trick each and every time.

It became all-consuming, and I didn't care about anything except getting high. Savage was like ten when I got on that shit really bad. I had even went to Savion's house telling him I needed him to take his kids because I was struggling. He shut the door in my face after calling me every name in the book. When Savage was about fifteen, Savion was killed in a bloody street war. I lost all my bearings then and turned to the drugs heavily.

By the time I figured out just how fucked up I was, Savage and Kaliyah had been gone for quite some time. At that time, I didn't care about anything or anybody but myself. I felt like my heart was completely broken. Savion was the only man I had ever loved. He was the only man that ever made me feel the way he did. He was my first everything. I was literally lost without him.

Soon, all that mattered to me was getting high and nothing more. I wanted to be completely numb all the time, so I didn't feel the hurt in my chest. To be honest, I was still grieving because, despite it all, I never got closure. By the time I figured out what was going on, Savion had been buried already. That daughter of his wouldn't have let me go to the funeral no way with her confused ass. She was out here acting like a whole nigga but was a female. Shame on her for that shit.

After that happened, I didn't see my son until a few years later. By then I'd been hearing his name here and there in the streets. At least I knew he wasn't dead or in jail so, to me, he was doing alright for himself. When he came to see me, and I finally told him who his father was, that's when shit went downhill. He got buddy-buddy with Savion's confused ass daughter. Who the fuck names their kid Halo anyway? I even heard he got married.

It had been ten long ass years since I saw him. When I heard that his wife was having a baby, I hustled my ass off to find out what hospital she was in. When I showed up to make amends, his mother-in-law got the drop on me, and we ended up fighting in the damn hallway. She got lucky because she snuck me, but that's ok. I'ma get her ass back next time. I was determined now more than ever to get my relationship back right with my son and daughter. They're all I got left in this world.

I knew I was a fucked up individual for how I fell off and didn't take care of them the right way, so I wanted to fix that. I was sure that if I got Savage to come around, then Kaliyah would too! I missed my babies something terrible. I was gonna take my ass to rehab and fix all this shit. I deserved to be in my grandbaby's life just as much as Savage's mother-in-law did.

Knowing that I was about to fix myself up, I tried to call Savage. I had gotten his number from one of these lil' niggas off the block because they thought I was tryna buy some work. Fuck they thought? I dialed his number and waited patiently for him to answer.

*"Speak,"* his voice boomed through the phone.

*"Kavion, baby, please don't hang up."*

*"Yo, who the fuck is this calling me baby?"*

I heard his wife in the background going the fuck off, so I tried to diffuse the shit quick.

*"It's your mama, and I wanted to talk to you."*

*"Mama? Nah, I ain't got one of those, but I do have an egg donor named Shae."*

*"Kavion, have some respect! I'm still your mother."*

*"And you're still the bitch that left me to fend for myself and my little sister so you could get high. The fuck you thought this was? You thought I'd have some sort of moment and all would be forgiven? Fuck outta here! What the fuck do you want, man?"*

*"Please, I just wanted to let you know that I'm sorry, and I'm going to rehab. I want to make things right with you and Kaliyah. I want to be a grandmother. I want my family back."* I broke down crying.

*"Yeah, shit sounds nice, but I don't believe your ass worth shit. Get the fuck off my line."*

Savage hung up on me, and I was beyond hurt. After all this time I was putting in an effort to correct my mistakes, but he didn't care. At least I wanted to try, right? I was going to check myself into rehab. I was gonna get the relationship back with my kids. I was gonna be an amazing grandma, on Monday though. Right now, I was gonna smoke my shit and get higher than a fucking kite. Savage's words cut me deep, and I needed to be numb from the shit right now.

# CHAPTER TWENTY-FIVE
## SAVAGE

Here comes this damn lady calling me and almost getting me cut by my damn wife. As soon as I asked who the fuck it was calling me baby, Royalty pulled a razor from God knows where and was 'bout to slice my ass the fuck up. When I said, it was my mama she calmed down but stood right next to me to hear the conversation. I saw now that Royalty really wasn't playing when she said she'd kill me. She low-key had me scared as fuck.

I listened to my mama yap about much of nothing. She claimed she was gonna get clean, but I'd believe it when I saw that shit. I wasn't listening to her talk. I wanted to see that action. Until then, her ass would be Shae the crackhead, not my mama, Ms. Faulk. I couldn't even call her a mother for all the shit me, and Kaliyah went through. I was just glad that shit wasn't worse than her smoking when we were younger. At least she wasn't one of those fiends that would sell her kids. I guess her funky ass had some kinda morals about herself.

"So, what all did she say?" Royalty asked.

I looked at her ass like she had two heads. "My nigga, you was ear hustling like a muthafucka. You heard everything."

"Don't get cut, my dude. Now I asked nicely. What did she say?"

"She said some shit about wanting to make shit right with us. I'm good on that shit. She can keep it to herself. Me nor Kaliyah don't give a fuck no more."

"I might not like her ass or the shit you told me about her, but that's still your mom. I say give her a chance and see if she fucks up again. If she does, then say fuck her and mean it. Everybody deserves a second chance. I gave you one instead of cutting your dick off like I wanted to."

I grabbed my dick at the mention of her cutting it off. What kinda shit did I get myself into? I'd never cheat on Royalty again, but I didn't need her threatening to cut my dick off either.

"Aye woman, chill with that cutting shit. If you cut my dick off, then I can't do nothing for you."

"You can always show me what that mouth do. That shit won't get cut," she said, looking at me.

"You really are crazy. Who the fuck did I marry? You waited ten years to show me you crazy?"

"Nah, I've always been crazy. You just waited ten years to be a dumb ass 'cuz you got comfortable with me thinking I wouldn't step. Play with me if you want to again, and ya' mama gon' be contactin' yo' ass from the other side of this world. Have her ass summoning you up like you the ghost of Christmas past or some shit."

I gulped hard and took a long look at my wife. I knew she was serious, and I deserved her coming at me reckless. She was hurt, but she was right. I had gotten comfortable and thought I could do anything. Instead of me talking to my wife about the shit, I found comfort in another woman. Jay wasn't just any other woman either. I had done shit for her that should've been specifically for my wife. You woulda thought that after I saw True go through all the shit that he did, I would never be that stupid. Fat asses is tempting though. Not justifying shit, just saying.

"Bae, I've hurt you when I shouldn't have, and I'll spend the rest of my life making that shit. I'ma man, and I can admit that I fucked up. I can also admit that I'll never do anything to jeopardize us ever again. Can I please just love on my wife?" I asked pulling her into me.

She let me kiss her deeply, and next thing I knew, my dick was down her throat. She was sucking me off like she had a point to prove, but she really didn't. Royalty was everything and more. I felt fucked up that I'd hurt her the way that I did. If this taught me anything, it taught me that a short thrill wasn't worth the bullshit that came after it. I let Royalty do her thing as I stood there with my toes curling and damn near speaking in tongues.

"Oh shit, bae, I'm bouta cum."

And then she sucked in her cheeks and latched on to my dick like a vacuum. I never came so hard in my damn life. My knees buckled, and Royalty moved just as I fell to the ground. My heart was beating fast as shit. I was sure I was having a heart attack, and she just stood there laughing at me. I had to catch my breath before I could say anything.

"The fuck kinda demon possessed you just now? You ain't never suck my dick like that before. Gimme my soul you just snatched from my body. Got damn it. Fuck!"

I was laying on the bedroom floor trying to catch my breath, and Royalty was still laughing at me as she walked away. She came back out the bathroom with her phone in her hand. My dick was still hanging out semi-hard with my shorts around my damn ankles. She snapped a picture while I lay there incapacitated. I was so glad all this shit was funny to her. As soon as I got the feeling back in my legs, I was gonna make her pay for that shit. Can you believe she left me on the floor? Didn't help a nigga up or nothing. My phone rang again, and I struggled to get up and answer it.

*"Hello?"* I asked, still outta breath.

*"Awww hell nah! I know you didn't answer the phone while y'all was having sex. That's just so damn nasty.*

*Meanwhile, your son over here eatin' me out of house and home right now."*

"*He's only like seven months old. How the hell is that even possible?"* I laughed.

"*I done introduced his extra hungry tail to table food, and now he can't get enough. I just sent your worrisome ass wife a video of him eating mashed potatoes."*

"*You still got your daughter blocked?"* I was dying laughing.

"*Sure in the fuck do. She ain't about to worry me twenty times a day like I ain't raised her ass. I swear you need to knock her up again or get her ass a hobby. She stays working my nerves calling me every time I have Sir. You should get her a kindle and tell her to read. That's what I do in my spare time."*

"*Stop going in on my baby like that. What's my son doing anyway?"*

"*Besides attacking this bowl of mashed potatoes, nothing. He's making a damn mess and laughing about the shit. Every time I tell him no, he smiles that gummy lil' smile, and I give in all over again. Make sure y'all next baby ugly so I don't wanna keep him or her all the time."*

"*What?"* I was laughing so hard at my mother-in-law. "*How the hell I'm 'posed to do that shit?"*

"*I don't know, but figure it out, or y'all will never*

*have y'all kids. I gotta go. Your son is throwing his food around like he pays for the groceries 'round here. Fucking with him all my edges gon' be snatched out. Lord help me."*

Mama James hung up, and I was still laughing hard as fuck. That woman was crazy as hell, but I loved her like she was my own mama. In a way, she was because she always gave me the best advice and kept it real at all times. That's what a mom was supposed to be. Not the egg donor I came from. She's lucky that nothing ever happened to me or Kaliyah while she was on that shit because I wouldn't have hesitated to body her ass if need be.

I finally got my ass all the way up and went looking for Royalty to repay the favor. I found her laying on the couch snoring lightly. I knew that looking after me and Sir was a lot. I appreciated the fuck outta my wife. I just had to show her better. Once I came up with a plan, I was taking her on a vacation to somewhere exotic so we could work on another baby. I wanted a daughter that looked just as beautiful as her mama.

I crept over to the couch careful not to make a sound. All she had on was one of my shirts, so I slid that shit up and started kissing on her thighs. She moved slightly, but she didn't wake up. I dipped my tongue into her pussy and massaged her clit with my hand. She moaned, so I kept doing what I was doing. Soon, I had my arms clamped down on her legs so she couldn't buck away from the oral assault I was putting on her pussy.

"Ssssss, fuck! Right there, bae, just like that. Ohmygod! This shit feels so got damn good!" Royalty yelled out.

"You gon' cum all over my face for me?"

"Mmmhmmm. Shit!"

I slurped her clit into my mouth and started humming. She bucked up at me, but I held her down as best as I could. I started talking into her pussy telling her I liked hot wet it was getting. Royalty started going crazy. She grabbed the back of my head and pushed my face so deep into her pussy. I was loving that shit. I went harder on her slipping a finger into her dripping wet hole. She came with a high-pitched scream. Now it was her turn to lay there breathless. I got up using my hand to wipe my face. She had squirt all down my chest too. I loved that wet shit.

"Got yo' ass back. It ain't funny now, is it?" I asked her.

"Fuck you, Kavion."

"Oh, I'm 'bout to."

I dropped my shorts and got down on my knees pulling her to the edge of the couch. She done fucked up now. I slid my thick dick into her pussy and moaned. Damn, her shit was extra tight. I loved the way her pussy hugged me like a second skin. I hit her with a few slow strokes before going to town on her ass. By the time I was done, we were sitting, and she was about to pass out. I did my job and fell out next to her. Whew! That was some fire ass pussy.

# CHAPTER TWENTY-SIX
## ROYALTY

Kavion wasn't slick coming in here tryna be sneaky. That's why I played sleep on his ass, but I did not expect him to work me like he did. I could tell that he was fucking me like he had a point to prove, but I didn't let that bother me. He was my first, my last, and my only, even if I wasn't his. I let him take those thoughts away with every lick of my pussy. I came so damn hard that I was sure I would see stars, and my ears would ring. Head was a powerful ass thing, especially when it's done right.

My husband and I made love once again and fell asleep on the couch. I only woke up because my phone was going off. I grabbed it, careful not to wake Kavion up. He was grumpy if somebody woke him up before he was ready. I answered the phone and whispered into it.

*"Hello?"*

*"Chile, why the hell you whisperin'? I'm sure Savage can hear you any way. What time y'all comin' to get this greedy lil' baby. He done ate all my food up."*

*"Mama, stop. Sir is just a baby. There's no way he's eating that much."*

*"Yeah, ok. Don't believe me, but watch me when I say*

*he's gonna start pulling shit off your plate soon. Speaking of babies, I talked to yo' husband. Y'all can't have no more pretty lil' babies. You won't ever have them because I will."*

"How am I supposed to stop that from happening, Mama? How, Sway?"

"How who? Who the hell is Sway?"

"It's just an expression, Mama," I said, laughing at her.

"Well, whoever the hell he is, is his ass single? You know Mama gotta have a life too."

"Oh my God! I can NOT with you right now. Lemme shower, and I'll be on my way to get my baby. I'll see you in a lil' bit, Mama. Kiss my baby for me." I chuckled.

"Yeah, yeah, I'll see you soon."

I went to my room and got my things together to take a shower. I didn't bother waking Kavion up because he looked like he needed the sleep. I knew this whole thing with that girl's mother was taking a toll on him. Although I didn't like the circumstances, I vowed to stand by my husband. I washed up quickly and quietly before slipping on my clothes and grabbing my keys.

"Fuck you think you goin' without me?" Kavion said, scaring the shit outta me.

"Damn bae, I thought you were still asleep."

"I was until I heard you whispering on the phone. You lucky you said something about my son, otherwise, I'd think you was on your way to do some bald-headed hoe shit. I woulda killed yo' ass for that."

"You already know I ain't you. This pussy is only reserved for one damn person. If it ain't Kavion Faulk, then ain't nobody getting' it. I ain't passin' my pussy out like penny candy the way you doin' your dick."

"But you was just creaming all over this dick a minute ago. You can't be mad and take my dick. Kinda shit is that?"

"I needed some dick. So what?" I shrugged. "If I can't get it from my husband, then I don't want it. Sorry to burst your lil' thot bubble, but I ain't the hoes you fuck with." I snapped at my husband.

He rubbed his hand down his face. I could tell he was frustrated, but I didn't give a damn. Just because we'd been having sex didn't give him the right to question me about a got damn thing. He had a point to prove, not me. I pushed past his ass and headed for the door.

"Go get my son and come straight home. I just wanna be under my family."

"Yeah, a'ight," I responded.

Without another word, I was in the wind. Kavion had me fucked up thinking he could throw demands around like he was running shit. If there was anything I learned in life, it was that when a nigga fucked up, the woman held all the cards. I'd be home when the fuck I got there. Kavion wasn't going nowhere. I could bet my life on it.

\*\*\*

"Hey, Mama. Where's my fat man at?"

"After his ass done ate up all his food and mine, I washed him up and put him down for a nap. Whew, that boy can eat. I hope yo' next child don't eat like that, otherwise I'ma need a food allowance when I watch them."

"Why you keep sayin' somethin' about a next child? I'm still tryna get used to the one I got. I ain't givin' Kavion another baby no time soon."

"That's what ya' mouth says, but your hips say something different. They spreadin' again, and the fact that Sir is doing shit like eating whole meals and pushing up on my furniture means he's moving his ass out the way."

"Yeah, ok. Like hell," I responded rolling my eyes.

There was no way in hell I was about to have another damn baby when Sir wasn't even a year old yet. Shit, I was still tryna deal with the shit Kavion had done. I wasn't the type of bitch to ever be short of self-esteem, but I'd be lying if I said what he did didn't fuck with my ego. I tried to find any fault in myself or what I was doing that would make my husband stray, but I found none. He was just doing shit just to do shit, and that's what fucked with me the most. Was he that comfortable with me that he thought he could do whatever he wanted, and I wouldn't go anywhere? Just thinking about it pissed me off all over again.

I sat down and talked to my mama until my baby woke up. I heard him making all sorts of noises over the baby monitor my mama had in the living room. I went into the room he had there and opened the door. As soon as Sir saw me, he got really excited. He started bouncing up and down and smiled with drool dripping from his mouth. I picked up my happy baby and changed him before taking him downstairs. My mama was in the kitchen cooking dinner, so I went to let her know we were leaving.

"Alright Mama, kiss this boy so we can go. I can already tell he's full of energy. Guess who's gonna be staying up with you tonight, lil' boy? Not ya' mama. That's right," I said, tickling my son.

His laugh was so infectious that me and my mama laughed with him. After she loved up on my son, we left. As I drove home, I kept thinking about whether or not I could really and fully trust Kavion again. I did take vows for better or worse, but I wasn't about to be dealing with the worse ten years in to this shit. Niggas fucked up in the beginning of a relationship, not ten years later--except my husband, my husband wanted to be the dummy.

By the time I got home, Sir was asleep again. I parked and got out before carefully lifting him out his car seat. Damn, he was heavy as shit. I was gonna have to remind my mama to stop feeding his ass every time he opened his mouth. I pressed the button for the elevator and waited. I hoisted Sir up on my shoulder and willed the elevator to hurry the fuck up. The bell dinged, and the doors opened up. I stepped inside and pressed the button for my floor.

I was exhausted and wanted to just climb into my bed with my husband and son. I got to our door and opened it with my key. I heard the hum of the television and something else. It sounded like somebody was talking loudly and didn't give a fuck who heard. That nigga better not be! I would be hotter than fish grease! I put my son in his bed and crept quietly to the bathroom door and put my ear to it.

*"Nigga, I said keep that crazy bitch in sight. I don't know what the fuck she's on, but now both of her daughters are gone. Ain't no tellin' what she might try to do now. She swears I'm responsible for both her daughters dying. I just got back in good with my wife. I don't need no more smoke,"* Savage said into the phone on the other side of the door.

I breathed a sigh of relief. I was about to be mad again. That let me know that I wasn't over this whole situation, and I didn't know when I would be, honestly. Just that fast I thought my husband was cheating again. *Get it together, sus,* I said to myself. It was gonna be a long road, but I knew that with time, we'd be good.

# CHAPTER TWENTY-SEVEN
## LANA

I was about tired of trying to track this bitch down. It had been over a week since I last talked to Shae about Savage. I was blowing up her damn phone and sending her all types of text messages, but she wasn't answering. I guess that's what happens when you give a crackhead five grand up front for some shit. I shoulda just gave her ass a stack and let that be that, but the shit was too easy. I tried calling her one more time, and she finally answered.

*"Damn bitch, it's about fucking time. I been callin' ya' ass for a week. Where the fuck you at?"*

*"Would you calm yo' ass the fuck down? You think I can just answer the phone whenever you call? How the fuck I'm 'posed to get information with my phone to my ear all the damn time? You fuckin' blowin' me right now."*

*"Well, did you find anything out while you talkin' all that shit?"*

*"I did. I'll be by that way later to let you know what all I got. I'll be there around nine. Have my drink ready."*

*"Yeah, yeah."*

I hung up excited as fuck that Shae came through. I

didn't even bother tryna figure out what she found out. I waited this long for information on that lil' nigga so I could wait a lil' longer. I decided to cook me a steak and some shrimp, smoke a blunt, and have a cold glass of Apple Crown to calm my nerves till Shae got here. By the time nine o'clock rolled around, I was nice and lit. There was a knock on my door, and I sauntered to it.

"Who is it?"

"It's Shae. Open the damn door."

I opened the door, and Shae pushed past me to get in.

"Damn, you rude bitch. Coulda at least said excuse me."

"Whatever. Where my drink at?"

"Lemme go make it for you now."

I walked off to make Shae's drink and smiled. I was about to have this bastard by the balls. He just didn't know. I fixed myself another drink before grabbing Shae's and going back into the living room. I passed her the drink. I took a huge gulp and stared at Shae.

"Well?" I asked impatiently.

"Well what, bitch?"

"The fuck did you find out?"

Shae picked her glass up again and took a drink before answering me. That's when I noticed this bitch had on some damn gloves, and it was almost eighty degrees outside.

Oh well, that's some crackhead shit, and that's what she was.

"Damn, a bitch can't even enjoy her drink. You just wanna jump straight into some shit. Can I enjoy my drink first? Shit."

"Yeah, a'ight. You just better be ready to tell me what the fuck I wanna know about that lil' nigga."

We sat and sipped our drinks watching the television aimlessly. A few minutes later, Shae snapped me out of my thoughts.

"Can I get a refill on this? That shit was good as fuck. Make it the same way," she said, handing me her glass.

I took the glass and held it like it had a disease. This bitch had the nerve to be wearing some red lipstick too. It didn't matter because I was gonna throw the glass in the trash the same way I did last time she was here.

When I came back and handed Shae her drink, she was leaned back on the couch all relaxed and shit. I hoped this bitch at least did a lil' something for herself with the money I was giving her besides smoking that shit up. She was sitting in front of me looking like a hot ass mess. Her wig looked like it had seen better days about twenty years ago, that lipstick was horrible, and she was ashy as fuck.

"I found out that Savage has been laying low. He's been staying in a condo on Lake Shore Drive, but it's the type of place that they call the resident before you're allowed to go to their place. Neither you nor I can get in there without being seen. Word on the street though is he has a business meeting coming up in a few days because he plans on selling his club. I heard some dude named Judas is supposed to be buying it. He's another dope boy from the south side. Anyway, the whole deal is supposed to go down in three days around eleven o'clock that night. Security might be tight, but it's probably the best way you can get to him. Now, can I get the rest of my money so I can go? I got shit to do."

I picked my drink up and took a large gulp. "Where the fuck you gotta go? To get high? Girl, hush. Lemme finish my drink, and I'll get yo damn money so you can go."

I finished my drink off and got up to go get this money. I got dizzy for a second and almost fell. Damn, I need to stop making my drinks so strong. I went into my room and into the closet where I pulled the stack of money out of an old purse. I walked slowly back into the living room my body feeling extremely heavy.

"You ok, Lana? You ain't lookin' too good," Shae asked me.

I heard her, but it sounded like an echo. I tossed the money to her and flopped down on the couch. I was out like a light before she was even all the way off her seat. When I woke up, it was night time. I tried to stretch, but I realized I couldn't. That's when I noticed that I was tied up. What the fuck?

"Nice of you to finally join me again. That steak and shrimp was good by the way. I always loved when you used to cook when we were younger."

"What the fuck is this about, Shae? If it's money you want, then I have more. You ain't gotta hurt me to rob me. Money ain't shit to me now."

"Is that what you think this is about? Money? My people got money. I don't need shit from you!" Shae hissed at me.

"Bitch, Savion is gone! Them drugs musta fucked you up real bad because that was the only money train yo' ass ever had."

"Nah, you forgot about the kids we had too. One of them was a lil' boy. A lil' boy I named Kavion. In the streets, he's known as Savage."

Recognition crossed my face, and that's when I knew I fucked up. This whole damn time I'd been dealing with the enemy. This bitch sat in my face acting like she was gonna help me when the whole time she was on bullshit.

"Did you really think I'd give up my own son to you? Ain't no fucking way!"

"He took my daughters from me! I know he's the

reason they're dead. Fuck him and fuck you too! You better whoop my ass something serious, otherwise I'ma fuck you up!" I yelled at her trying to intimidate her.

Shae turned around and picked up a small bag. I didn't even notice that her ass had brought a bag in with her. My eyes went wide as she started pulling shit out her bag. She had a small baggie of white powder, an old spoon, a lighter and a syringe. She set her shit up neatly on the table. I started to scream, and she punched me hard as fuck in the mouth. It knocked the wind out of me. She roughly stuffed a rag in my mouth. I thought I was gonna choke on the blood that was pooling in my mouth.

I struggled to get loose when she started soaking up the liquid in the syringe. I knew this bitch liked to get high, but if I could get out of these restraints, then I could whoop her ass while she was on that shit. It shouldn't be hard to fight a crackhead, right?

"You can make all the noise you want, hoe. Ain't nobody coming to save you. Both of your daughters are dead, and I'm 'bout to send you to hell right along with them," Shae said, walking over to me with the syringe.

She roughly grabbed my arm and jabbed the syringe into it. I tried to jerk free from her grasp, but it was no use. I felt the swoosh of the liquid into my arm. It took all of two minutes for the shit to kick in. I felt like I was floating for a lil' bit then my heart started beating really fast. I couldn't breathe, and it had nothing to do with the gag in my mouth. My eyes rolled in the back of my head, and I started shaking.

A bitch really died of an overdose in her living room. I couldn't do shit about it now though, could I? How the fuck I let a crackhead get the best of me?

# CHAPTER TWENTY-EIGHT
## HALO

I was hoping that this shit with Savage would die the fuck down. Bruh had already dealt with more than enough shit. That's what his dumb ass gets though. I told him before to never mix business with pleasure. True told him the same damn thing before he bought the club. Dumb ass just couldn't resist a fat ass.

Speaking of fat asses, currently, Anisa was asleep with her ass high in the air. I had worked that ass out. She kept sending me pictures of her in sexy lil' outfits and pussy shots. Talk about making a muthafucka want you. Anisa was on point with all her shit. I thought I loved shorty. Nah, scratch that. I knew I loved shorty, and it was time to make it official. She had already met my baby, so now it was time to introduce her to the family. Savage called me saying we needed to get together soon, and I agreed.

I left my bedroom so I wouldn't wake Anisa up. It was a Saturday, and it was early as fuck. I checked the time to see it was a lil' past six. I decided to make breakfast for my ladies. I pulled the turkey bacon out the refrigerator along with some turkey sausage patties. My girls liked bacon, but I liked sausage. I grabbed the eggs, milk, powdered sugar, butter, bread, and biscuits. I was gonna make French Toast to go with the eggs, sausage, and biscuits.

I laid everything on the counter and washed my hands before starting up. I whipped up the eggs really good for both batches I needed. One would be for the bread for the French Toast, and the other would be for us to eat. Once the pans were on the stove and ready to go, I poured the eggs in one pan and placed two pieces of battered bread on the other one. I had the kitchen smelling really good when Anisa crept up on me.

"Good morning, baby. It smells really good up in here. Lemme find out you tryna make me fall in love." She giggled before placing a kiss on my lips.

"That's 'cuz a nigga really does love you," I replied.

Anisa's eyes went wide as hell, and she didn't say shit. She just stood there looking at me like a deer caught in some headlights. I wondered if I had said the wrong thing to her, but I didn't have to wait long to find out.

"Uhhh Halo, we need to talk," she said nervously.

"What's good then?" I said defensively.

"I really like you and all, but this is my first time ever being with a woman. I never planned on being with a woman ever in my life, but this just happened with you."

"Fuck is you really sayin', shorty?"

"I'm saying I can't love you back. I wanna get married and have babies. I can't do that with you. My family would never accept it, accept us."

"You think we can't do that shit? It's lesbians having babies and getting married all the damn time now. Who gives a fuck who don't like it? I introduced you to my daughter, and that shit was hard to do. I don't bring nobody but family around her. You're the first person I've been with like this since her mother died."

"I'm sorry, Halo. I really am. Let me get my things, and I'll go," Anisa said with tears in her eyes.

I was trying hard as fuck not to show my emotions, but it was tough. I was ok, but when Baby Storm walked in and said what she said, I couldn't hold back.

"My Halo, is Anisa leaving? She doesn't want us anymore?" she asked crying.

That was it for me. I cut the stove off, scooped my daughter in my arms, and held her tight. We both cried as we stood in the kitchen. I felt like I was in mourning all over again. This was the first time I had opened up to having another relationship, and this shit happened. I felt bad as fuck, but I felt even worse that I had brought my daughter into it. I never let her meet anybody I dealt with after Storm passed away because they were just something to do. I wasn't serious about anybody until I got with Anisa.

As we stood in the kitchen, me still holding onto Baby Storm, Anisa came down the stairs with her bags packed. She looked at me with sad eyes, but I mugged the fuck outta her. This bitch was foul, and she knew it. How the fuck she start a whole damn relationship with me knowing she was a fake ass lesbian? That shit had me hotter than fish grease. I didn't say shit to her as she placed her key on the hallway table and left. I stroked my daughter's back consoling her. I knew she was hurt, but so was I. Fuck love!

***

I ended up making us breakfast, and over breakfast, I explained to my daughter that everything would be ok. She understood because she was really smart for her age. I was mad at myself for allowing this to happen. I had no idea that Anisa would flip on me the way she did. I thought we were building some shit. I meant it when I said I didn't introduce Baby Storm to everybody. You know how much pussy I've had in the last nine years? More than enough, but none of them bitches were worth a relationship.

I was off bitches for a while. Fuck a while. I'd be off bitches till Baby Storm graduated and moved out. Maybe then I'd hit an island or two and find me a foreign bitch. Shit was what it was. After breakfast, me and my baby just pigged out with junk food and Netflix. It was just one of those types of days. As I was getting up to go use the bathroom, my doorbell rang. I wondered who the fuck it was because nobody but my family came over here.

"Yo, who is it?" I barked.

"Please, open the door. I need to talk to you," a female's voice came back.

I snatched the door open not knowing what to expect, but I damn sure didn't expect Savage's mama to be on my doorstep.

"Fuck you want?" I snapped.

"I know I'm not somebody you want to talk to, but I need your help."

"Why the fuck would I help you?"

"Because it's about Savage."

Reluctantly, I let her funky ass in. Hell no she wasn't my favorite person in the world. I still blamed her ass for my mother killing herself. She just couldn't stay away from my pops. I knew it wasn't right to blame her and not my father, but shit, my mother didn't kill herself until this crazy bitch showed up at our house all them years ago. I was gonna give her ass five minutes to explain why she was there before I put her out. I told my daughter to go to her room for a bit, and I'd call her when she can come back out.

"Talk. You got five minutes."

"I'ma need more than that, but I'll explain as much as

I can."

I listened as she told me about how she knew Lana and how Lana had called her to help her take down Savage. She went on and on about how she was trying to play it off like she'd help her and even took some money from her to make it legit. She told me she took the money and checked into an outpatient rehab facility. She needed to be back by six every evening, so she didn't have a lot of time to do shit.

"So, I hear all that shit you sayin', but you ain't told me nothin' I don't know already besides you knowin' the bitch."

"Well, the bitch is dead. Tell my son that I really wanna have a relationship with him. That's why I checked into rehab. That's why I handled his problem for him. I just want another chance. I'll go now."

I couldn't just let her leave like that. Even though I didn't like her, I appreciated the fuck outta her for handling that shit for my brother.

"Aye!"

She spun around quickly. "Yeah?" she asked.

"Good looking out. You need a ride or anything?"

"Nah, I'm good. Just do me a favor--don't tell Savage none of this. I wanna be the one to tell him. I wanna prove myself to him again."

"You got that."

I closed the door behind Ms. Faulk and just stood there in shock. Check that shit out. I didn't expect her to say no shit like to me, but who the fuck was I to judge? I would keep that shit like she asked me. After all, it wasn't my place to say anything anyway.

# CHAPTER TWENTY-NINE
## ROYALTY

I woke up feeling like shit. My head was pounding, my titties were sore, and my lower back felt like I had been drop kicked in it. I got up to use the bathroom, and the smell of the soap that lingered in the air made me gag. I dropped to my knees and hugged the toilet. I literally threw up everything and then dry heaved after that. It took all the energy I had to get up and brush my teeth. Why the fuck did I do that? I ended up throwing up again.

"Arghhhh! This shit can't be happening," I said out loud.

Kavion came running into the bathroom to see what was wrong because he heard me scream out.

"You good, bae?"

"Nan, nigga. I ain't good. I think it's something I ate."

"Or a real nigga knocked you up again," he said smirking.

"If you knocked me up again with another one of your big-headed ass babies, I want a new house, a 2020 model Maybach as a push gift, and for you to sell that damn club."

"Done, done, and done," he sai,d marking them off with his fingers.

"I got a meeting in a few days to sell the club anyway. I don't want no more smoke from you, especially when you quotin' *Hail Mary* lyrics and shit. Some nigga named Judas from out south hit me up about buying it."

"Good. Now, since you think I'm pregnant, go to the store and get me a test."

"Say less."

Kavion flew out the door, and I heard it slam behind him. I tried to get up on weak knees and just rinsed my mouth out with some water. I walked slowly back to my bed and laid down. My body felt so messed up. I already knew that I was pregnant again, but that test would confirm it. Was I ready for another baby? Our son wasn't even a year old yet. I shook my head because even if I wasn't ready, this baby was coming. It didn't even feel like Kavion had been gone long before he was right back in the room with me.

"She's having my baby, and it means so much to me. There's nothing more precious than to raise a family. Oooooh yeah!" Kavion crooned.

"Shut yo dumb, wanna be K-Ci ass the fuck up and gimme that test."

"Ooooh, you is mean, girl. I'ma tell yo' mama on

you."

"Stop playin' with me, bruh. I don't feel good, and you wanna joke. Help me up."

Kavion did as I asked him to. We went back into the bathroom, and with shaky hands, I opened the box with the test in it. I pissed on the end of the stick, put the cap on it, and laid it on the sink. I wiped, flushed, and washed my hands. Barely a minute went by when two bright pink lines popped up.

"Yesssss! A nigga done did that shit again. Lemme go call my people!" Kavion yelled excitedly as he pulled his phone from his pocket.

I climbed back in my bed and decided to call my mama to get it out the way. I dialed her number and waited for her to answer.

*"Hello chile, what you want? You just came and got your baby, so I know you not tryna bring him back just yet."*

*"You were right, Mama."*

*"Come again? What you talkin' 'bout?"*

*"I'm pregnant again. I just took a test."*

*"I told you. I told you, but did you wanna listen to me? Nooooooo, of course not. It ain't like I ain't never had a child, watched children, had a whole career taking care of children, taking care of my gran—"*

*"I get it, Mama, damn."*

*"Who you cussin' at lil' girl? I will drive over there and whoop yo' ass. You still ain't too old to catch these hands."*

*"Sorry, Mama. I'm just frustrated. I wasn't expecting this."*

*"Well, that sounds much better. What did you expect when you and your husband been humpin' like rabbits? How y'all young kids say it nowadays? You was bustin' it wide open or whatever?"*

*"Bye, Mama. I am NOT doing this with you right now,"* I said laughing.

*"But did it make you laugh?"*

*"It did."*

*"Good. Then I did my job. Love you, baby, and get some rest."*

*"Love you too."*

I hung up with my mama feeling a little better. I snuggled under the blanket and was out like a light. Kavion woke me up a few hours later with some food. He brought a tray into the room with some orange juice, a cinnamon raisin bagel, some chicken soup, and crackers. I ate slowly because I was scared I was gonna throw everything up, but I didn't. I was feeling way better than I did earlier. I asked Kavion to bring me Sir so I could spend time with my baby.

He left out the room and returned shortly with our son. As soon as I had Sir in my arms, he just busted out crying. I tried to console him even getting up and walking the room with him, but nothing helped. I tried to feed him, and he didn't even want to latch on. Kavion brought me a bottle, but he wouldn't take it. He didn't have a fever or anything, so it made me worried.

"Here, let me try, bae."

I handed Sir over, and as soon as he was in his father's arms, he went quiet. Kavion tried giving him the bottle, and he took it with no problems. That all made me feel some kind of way. Why didn't my baby want me? Was it my pregnancy? Was that the reason why? I climbed back in bed with my feelings hurt. Kavion fed and changed Sir before putting him back to sleep. He climbed into bed with me afterwards.

"It's gonna be ok, shorty. I love you, and I always got you. Don't even trip off how Sir is acting. You know they say kids can sense pregnant folks and all that other shit. He'll come around."

I just shook my head as I snuggled up with my husband. Within minutes, I was out like a light again. Visions of babies danced in my head, and I smiled at the thought. I couldn't wait to have this baby.

# CHAPTER THIRTY

## SAVAGE

Once I was sure that my wife was asleep again, I slipped out of bed and headed into the living room. I couldn't believe I was 'bout to be a daddy again. Shit was wild. I was hoping for another son, but with the way God was set up, he'd give me a daughter just to be cruel. I had already called all my folks, so they knew what was up. Honesty damn near talked my head off about how she had to come up here again. I told bro to keep her ass down there until my seed was born. I didn't want the extra headache.

I rolled a blunt, but I wouldn't smoke it in the house. Royalty would kill my ass if she so much as smelled weed in the house. Her sensitive nose having ass. I stepped out on the balcony and lit up. A nigga felt like he was on top of the world right now. The only thing I had to worry about was Lana's worrisome ass, but with our upcoming court date, I hoped to get rid of all that bullshit. Now that was one crazy ass bitch. She needed to be in somebody's looney bin.

As soon as I took a toke on my blunt, my phone rang. I didn't recognize the number, so I ignored the call. Minutes later, my phone rang again. I ignored it again. When my phone rang for the third time, I said fuck it and answered it.

*"Who the fuck is this?"* I barked into my phone.

*"Kavion, please don't hang up. It's me."*

*"Only one muthafuckin' person gets to call me Kavion, and that ain't you. What the fuck you want, Shae?"*

*"Look, I want to make amends. I really want a relationship with you, your sister, and my grandbaby. Please Kavion, let me apologize. I was wrong, and I know I was wrong all those years ago. Better late than never, right?"*

*"What? Are you dying or some shit? That's the only time a muthafucka wanna get right with the people they fucked over before."*

*"I'm not dying, but I realized when I was approached with some bullshit recently that I would still do what a mother does for her kids."*

*"Like you know what the fuck it is to be a mother. You ain't ever did shit for me or Kaliyah after Pops was killed. Fuck you mean you'll do what a mother does for her kids? Explain that dumb shit you talkin'."*

*"I'd rather not say over the phone. Can we meet somewhere, please? I'm begging you."*

*"I'll meet you, but you got less than ten minutes to get ya' point across, or I'm out. I don't have time for the bullshit."*

*"Thank you, son."*

*"You don't get to do that. You don't get to call me son. You have to earn that shit back, and you ain't done it yet."*

I hung up the phone not really knowing how to feel. I sucked that shit up and went to tell Royalty where I was going. She asked me if I wanted her to go with me, but I knew this was some shit I had to do alone. I'd get up with my lil' sister later and fill her in on whatever our egg donor told me. I know y'all probably looking at me and thinking why am I even giving this broad a chance, right? Well, shit, she's still my mama, and even as a grown ass man, sometimes I still want my mama. I held onto a grudge long enough, so I was gonna hear her out.

Since I told her to meet me at Montrose Beach which wasn't too far from where I lived, I left our building and walked over there. I knew I'd get there before her. I lit my blunt back up on the walk since my shit went out earlier. I smoked and found a bench near the bait shop. I already shot her a text and let her know that's where I'd be. I waited patiently smoking till she got there. I knew I needed to be faded to be able to have a civil conversation with this woman.

Contrary to what a lot of people believed, a man's first love was his mother, the same way a daughter's first love was her father. Me and my sisters were robbed of that shit. I put that all on my mama because had she not noticed that she was fucking with a married man, we may have had half a chance to have a decent life. When Kalila left, Mama started tripping, and when Pops died, she went overboard. I literally had to fend for myself and Kaliyah. All that shit was stressful as a lil' nigga, but I made it do what it do. After I had been sitting there about twenty minutes, a silver Altima pulled up. I watched as Shae got out the car.

"Hey Kavion, how are you?"

"Yo, cut the shit, Shae. Say what you gotta say and be done with it. I really don't have time for bullshit."

"Ok, I can understand that. Can we sit in my car? What I got to say don't need to be heard by nobody but us."

I walked over to the car and got in the passenger seat. Once I was inside the car, she broke down how Lana called her, what she wanted her to do, and how she handled the whole thing. For once I was fuckin' speechless. There was no way I thought she'd ever come through for the kid the way she did. I was kinda stuck on what the fuck I was supposed to say, but she kept talking.

"I just want you to know that I did this because despite what you think, I do love you and both of your sisters. I do love my daughter-in-law and my grandson. I even love Halo because she's a part of Savion, and I loved that man with all of me. I'm sorry that his wife committed suicide, but that wasn't my fault what she did. She made that decision the same way I made that decision to fuck with drugs. I really and truly am sorry, Kavion. I just want you to forgive me. I've already got myself into rehab. I wanna do right by y'all. Please."

"I hear you, but you gotta prove that shit. I can hear a muthafucka talk all got damn day, but without no proof, shit don't mean not a muthafuckin' thing to me. I appreciate the shit you did for me when it came to Lana's ass, but that still don't solve the bullshit between us."

"Give me another month or two, Kavion. I'm gon' prove it to you. I promise."

I got out her car without another word. A nigga was still stuck on the fact that she fixed my lil' issue with Lana. I knew for a fact that that bird was gon' continue to give me problems. Even after our court date. I guess this bitch wouldn't show up for court, but at the same time, I wondered what kinda problems that would cause for me in the future. With Lana not showing up, the spotlight would be on me. I didn't need no extra ass heat.

I waited until Shae pulled the fuck off to walk back towards my house. I was stuck on the fact that I didn't even know what the fuck to do. I knew without a shadow of a doubt that I would tell my wife this shit, but I might need

Honesty to come through for a nigga one time. There was no way that CPD would let this shit just slide without picking me the fuck up. Ain't no fuckin' way!

# EPILOGUE
# SEVEN MONTHS LATER...
# SAVAGE

There was all kinds of speculation on me when Lana never showed up for court. Of course, CPD kept sniffing around my ass, but they didn't find shit. I was clean as a muthafuckin' whistle. Honesty made sure of that shit. That nigga Judas ended up buying the club, so I was 5.5 million dollars richer and had money to invest in whatever I wanted. I followed a nigga on social media, low-key, who told me about investing and making my money work for me. I bought a timeshare out in Jamaica and even had a summer home in Texas so I could visit my bro whenever I wanted to.

Halo ended up taking Baby Storm and moving to Cali. She said she needed a change of scenery. I couldn't fault her for that shit. I felt sis on that shit. Real talk, we were looking to move down south somewhere too. Maybe the Carolinas since a lot of our people were there. A nigga knew he could thrive there. I didn't even get to open my restaurant the way I wanted to in the Chi because of the drama.

Y'all wanna hear some funny shit? My mama actually went to rehab like she said she would. She was now almost one year sober. I had to reintroduce her to my wife and son while we waited on the arrival of our new baby. Royalty and I were having a lil' girl. Yeah, God was getting back at me for all the shit I done did to my wife. I was cool with it though. I was so ready to meet my princess. We already had a name picked out for her.

Currently, I was en route to Illinois Masonic Medical Center with Royalty screaming at me in the passenger seat. Sir was already with Mama James, and she was meeting us there. I had called my mama, Kaliyah, and even True and Honesty. They said they'd be on the next flight. Hopefully, they'd be here before the birth of my daughter. Halo got in last night, so her and Baby Storm were already at the hospital waiting on us.

I pulled into the emergency entrance, and Royalty barely let the car stop before she hopped out. I ain't never seen a pregnant woman run that damn fast before. She took off like the road runner in the old Saturday morning cartoons. It was funny, but it wasn't because I knew she was in a ton of pain. Halo told me she got her while I went to go park. Thank God for those expecting mother parking spots they had at hospitals now. I swerved into a spot and cut the engine.

One thing I had a hard time doing in my life was praying. Like seriously praying. I just didn't think that God looked out for people like me. On the off chance that he did,

I sent him up a lil' something.

"Dear God, if you're listening, please let my wife and baby be alright. I know I'm probably not your favorite person, but I love my family. You have truly blessed me when I didn't even think I could ever have all this. I ask for a safe delivery and a healthy baby. Thank you for all you've done for me. In your name, Amen."

I got out the car, hit the alarm, and jogged to the entrance. As soon as I walked in, it was pure pandemonium. I had to pull my mama and Mama James apart because they were standing toe to toe.

"Don't think you about to pull the shit you did last time. I'll whoop yo' ass again up in here. We in the right place for you to act up 'cuz they got plenty beds up in here," Mama James said to my mama.

"I'm different than I was a year ago but try me now and watch what the fuck happens. You better ask about me."

"Already did. Survey says you still a crackhead, hoe."

"MAN, ENOUGH! FUCK IS WRONG WITH Y'ALL? MY WIFE IS HAVING Y'ALL GRANDBABY, AND Y'ALL OUT HERE CUTTIN' THE FUCK UP! SIT Y'ALL ASSES DOWN! FUCK!" I hollered at both of them.

I was so fuckin' mad that I was shaking, but Halo took over, and I walked off. I went to the desk to check where my wife was, and they gave me her room number. I told the rest of the family to follow me and gave a look to my mama and Mama James to let them know I wasn't playing games. We all got in the elevator and headed upstairs. I was nervous as shit. Something didn't feel right, but I didn't know what it was. I shook that shit off though. It was time for me to be strong for my wife.

I left everyone in the waiting room and told both my mama and Mama James to follow me. Royalty and I had agreed that they could be in the room with us for the birth of our daughter. The minute either one of them decided to start acting up, I was kicking both their asses out. I didn't give a damn. My wife needed peace not problems. I took my spot at her side after washing my hands. She was sweating really hard. I grabbed her hand and coached her.

"You got this, bae. You can do it. Our baby is gonna be here in no time. Squeeze my hand as hard as you need to. I'm right here."

Now, why the fuck did I tell her ass that shit? She squeezed the fuck out my hand. I think she broke my shit. That's how bad my hand was hurting. I had no clue Royalty was that damn strong. I admired her for that strength though. As I stood by her side and watched her birth my daughter into this world, I had a newfound respect for my wife. With new life came new beginnings, and I felt like this was the start of something new for us. Hearing my daughter's cry for the first time made me break out in tears.

"She's here! Dad, do you want to cut the umbilical cord?" the doctor asked me.

I happily walked over to the prep area where they were cleaning my daughter up. You could already tell she looked just like her mama. She was screaming at the top of her lungs, but that was alright by me. I cut the cord and watched closely as they cleaned my baby up. Just as the nurse finished washing and swaddling her, there was a knock at the door. Mama James went to open the door, and her eyes got big as hell.

"The fuck? Can I help you?" she spat out, looking at our unwanted guests.

I looked at Royalty not knowing what to expect, and she was looking at me with tears in her eyes. Our entire room stopped what they were doing and gave the visitors all their attention. The doctor decided to step up and take the lead. The nurse placed my daughter in my arms hurriedly.

"Can I help you, fine gentlemen, today? This woman has just given birth. I'm sure we can step in the hallway and resolve whatever issue as necessary."

"My name is Detective Orman; this is Detective Rafael. We are here for Ms. Shae Faulk."

"That would be me," my mama said, stepping up.

I gave the baby to Royalty before stepping in front of my mama. "Mama, what's goin' on?"

"Just remember that I love you, son. You and Kaliyah both. I love both of my grandbabies too. Don't worry about an old woman like me. I've lived my life already. Now I want you to go live yours. Like really live, son. I love you."

My mama stepped around and walked over to the detectives. One of them pulled out handcuffs while the other one started to read my mama her rights. I was stuck. What the fuck was happening?

"Yo, what is all this shit about? I hear y'all reading her rights and shit, but what she gettin' charged with?"

"First-degree murder of Lana Morales. Second-degree murder of Jayonna and Tisha Morales. She'll have a bond hearing in the morning. I suggest you get her a lawyer."

They led my mama out the room, and I was floored. How in the fuck were they charging her for Jayonna and Tisha's murders? Both of those were accidents. I knew about Lana because my mama told me, but I hadn't told anyone. I heard screams from the waiting room, and I took off running out the room.

"Where the fuck y'all takin' my mama? What the fuck is going on? Where is my brother? Mama, tell me what's going on?" Kaliyah screamed.

I think every single nurse that was at the nurse's station were in tears watching Kaliyah break down the way that she did. She fell to her knees and was balling her eyes out. All I could do was grab my lil' sister and hold her while she cried. Halo shielded Baby Storm from what was going on. This was just way too fucking much, even for me. I nodded at Halo and mouthed Honesty's name, so she knew what to do. She nodded back and got on her phone immediately.

"C'mon Liyah, we stronger than this. We can make it through anything. I got you, and I got Mama. We gon' get past this just like we got past everything else in our way."

"We just got her back, Kavion. How they just gon' take her away like that when we just got her back? This is so fucked up."

I shushed her and held her tight. I finally got her to calm down, so I decided to go back and check on my wife. When I walked in, Royalty was nursing the baby. I never saw something more beautiful. I swear, I needed this positivity right now because my heart was breaking all over again. I walked over to the bed, and my wife looked up at me.

"You gonna be ok, bae?"

"I will be. You know me, I'ma thug," I said, laughing with tears threatening to fall from my eyes.

"Kavion baby, I really am sorry about what happened

with your mama. Forgive me for earlier."

"It's nothing, Mama James. I'ma work all this out, and she'll be back home in no time."

"Those are some serious charges though. Are you sure you can get a lawyer to handle that right away?"

"My best friend's wife is a lawyer. One of the best damn lawyers I know. If anybody can get my mama outta jail, it's her. I'm not worried. What I am worried about though, is the name for our lil' one. Did you tell her yet, bae?" I said, turning to Royalty.

"Tell me what? Y'all just keepin' me in the dark. What's her name gonna be?"

"Majesty Princess Faulk."

"That's so beautiful."

I looked back and forth between my wife, daughter, and mother-in-law. Even though my mama wasn't here, she was still with us in spirit. As we talked amongst ourselves and I rocked Majesty to sleep, True, and Honesty busted into the room. The bang of the door on the wall startled Majesty, and she started crying again. I calmed her down before placing her in Honesty's arms. She cooed at her, and I stepped into the hallway with True. He told me what Halo told him, and I filled in the rest. He let me know that Honesty made calls to a few people she knew. It was likely that my mama was gonna be held without bond. There wasn't shit we could do tonight, so I sent everyone home to my place and stayed with my wife and daughter.

***

"All rise. The Honorable Diane Riamor presiding. State of Illinois versus Shae Faulk. Docket number 100576. One count of first-degree murder. Two counts of second-degree murder. You may be seated."

True and I sat down as we watched Honesty step up to the podium. She was a beast in the courtroom, so I had no doubt about her skills.

"Your honor, my name is Honesty Thomas. I'll be Ms. Faulk's attorney. At this time, I'm requesting bail for my client. She's not a flight risk nor does she even have a passport. She barely has an identification card. These charges are ridiculous, and there should be no reason her bail should be denied," Honesty stated.

"As ridiculous as they may seem, Mrs. Thomas, they are very real and very punishable. Bail is denied because although Ms. Faulk may not have any resources, her son, Kavion Faulk, does. We don't need any mishaps to occur with these types of charges, so she will be remanded to Cook County Jail until trial. How does the defendant plead?"

"Guilty, your honor."

My mama wouldn't even look at me even though I

was burning a hole through the side of her head. This wasn't what we all discussed. She was supposed to plead not guilty and take it to trial where Honesty had a good chance of getting her off. They barely had any evidence. All they had was speculation. As a matter of fact, their whole theory was circumstantial.

"Your honor, may I have a moment with my client?" Honesty quickly stated.

"You may."

I saw Honesty arguing with my mama, but then my mama looked at me. She nodded her head at me, and I walked over to the edge of the aisle which was as far as I could go.

"Mama, what are you doing? This is what we talked about."

"They questioned the hell outta me while I waited for Honesty to come last night. They did it again after she left. They want you under the jail, son. I don't know what you've done in the streets nor do I care, but I love you enough to take this for you. You have two children that will need their father. Don't be like me and your daddy. Love those babies. Love your wife. Keep your family together the way I couldn't. I know you don't want me to do this, but this is my decision. Leave me be. I love you."

"But Mama, what about all we worked for? You went to rehab and everything. Just like that you're gonna throw everything away? How Mama? You know I love you too but, this ain't the way."

In that moment I felt like that lost lil' boy again who wondered where his mama went. It was that same feeling I got when I first got teased at school that my mama was a crackhead. It was the feeling I got when I first had to take care of Kaliyah. So many emotions ran through me, and the tears just flooded my eyes. I got up and walked back to my seat while my mama turned back to the judge.

"Mrs. Thomas, does your client's plea still stand or does it change?"

"It stands, your honor."

"An admission of guilt means to forego a trial. Does your client understand this, Mrs. Thomas?"

"Yes, your honor."

"So shall it be. The court finds Ms. Shae Faulk guilty of murder in the first degree on one count and guilty of second degree on two counts. I impose the maximum sentence for each count which is twenty years to life for count one and fifteen years to life on counts two and three. Defendant will be remanded to Cook County Jail and placed for movement to another facility when room becomes available. Do you understand these charges and sentences as they are being read to you, Ms. Faulk?"

"I do, your honor."

"Bailiff, please cuff Ms. Faulk and return her to holding for transport. This court is dismissed."

I was able to hug my mama one last time before they led her away. This was fucked up on so many levels. How could she choose to die behind bars after she fought so hard for her life this past year? I felt fucked up, and nobody could console me. We all left and went back to my condo. Once there, I relayed everything that happened to the rest of my family. Everybody was just as shocked as me. I broke everything down, and I even wanted to go turn myself in, but Kaliyah stopped me.

"No, bro. You're gonna do what Mama said. She owed us a life, and you were the one who gave it to us. She's just repaying that favor. All we can do now is make sure she's straight while she's in there. I love you, big brother. Always."

I pulled my sister in for a hug, and we stayed like for a long ass time. By the time I let her go, the room had cleared out. She went to her room, and I went in search for everyone else. I thanked True and Honesty for coming through again. Honesty apologized for not being able to help me more than she did. They left because they had a flight to catch, so I hugged them and sent them on their way.

"Aye yo, I know I blamed ya' mama for what my mama did but, seeing her turn her shit around made me look at shit differently too. My mama is always gon' be my mama, but she was a coward for what she did. She didn't have to kill herself. I just wanted somebody to place the blame on, and your mama was there. I'm sorry, bro. You got your mama still, so do what you can. I'd give anything to hug my mama one more time. Know that I always got your back. I love you."

"I appreciate that, Halo. We bumped heads at first, but I wouldn't trade you for the world. Thanks for always having my back. I love you too."

Halo took her daughter and left too. After I locked up behind everybody, I went in search of my wife and kids. I found them all in bed together. Royalty was asleep with Majesty cuddled in her arms. Sir was sitting on the bed watching Paw Patrol quietly. This was life. Actually, this was better than life. Second chances were everything, and I wasn't gonna ruin mine. It could have easily been me in jail for the rest of my life. Although I didn't want my mama to be in there, I understood her reasoning. Just goes to show you that a mother's love transcends any and everything. I was gonna do just what she said and live life. Now it was time to catch flights and love on my family. I'd never take them for granted again.

# THE END